I0760409

Following hot on the heels of his last adventure, everyone's favourite one-armed vengeance machine Micah 'Slow Bear' Cross makes his way to the Californian wine-country of the San Bernardino valley.

As you might expect, Slow Bear isn't there to take in the sunshine or enjoy a nice glass or two of red - he's got other things on his mind. Messier things. Bloodier things.

First on Micah's list is to pay a visit to a predatory child-trafficker he's tracked down to the Golden State and to extract some information to help in his continuing search for Lady (the kidnapped & trafficked long-lost love of his life).

Bloody chaos inevitably ensues, but has Slow Bear bitten off more than even he can chew this time?

This edition first published 2024 by Fahrenheit Thirteen, an imprint of Fahrenheit Press.

ISBN: 978-1-914475-77-1

10 9 8 7 6 5 4 3 2 1

www.Fahrenheit-Press.com

F 4 E

Slowest Bear

By

Anthony Neil Smith

Fahrenheit Thirteen

By the same author.

- *Slow Bear*
- *Slower Bear*
- *The Butcher's Prayer*
- *Trash Pandas*

Chapter 1

Micah "Slow Bear" Cross, exhausted and soaked in a kiddie-rapist's blood, slumped into a poolside lounge chair and fought to catch his breath. The meat mallet slipped from his solitary hand. He shook brain off his fingers.

The pedo in Speedos was floating facedown – funny way to put it since he didn't have much face left – the whole pool a bloom of ruby red.

It was quiet now. Hadn't been earlier, the pedo shouting for help until Slow Bear crushed his voice box. A pleasant late afternoon in San Bernardino, California. A chill in the air. Still spring? Or summer now? Even fall?

The pedo's mansion was a giant hilltop monstrosity with too many roof points, too many gilded bathrooms, too many bedrooms with four-post beds and too many overstuffed pillows you can't even use. Too much marble, too many fancy lights and chandeliers and etched glass.

Too many toys. Yep, toys.

Of both the blue and pink persuasions.

Of both the *child* and *adult* persuasions.

Because, remember: kiddie-rapist.

Slow Bear gave the kiddie-rapist a nickname: Shitfoot.

Not his given name of…oh, fuck it, Slow Bear thought. Dude's part in the story was done. He'd lost his rights to his real name.

Shitfoot it was.

Shitfoot drifted in the currents of the ruby red pool. No, not ruby red. Oxblood? Wine?

Nothing so elegant for Shitfoot. Red as hog's blood.

Luckily, Shitfoot had been at home alone in his speedos because he was expecting a delivery. A real live delivery. Two girls, one verging on teenhood, and the other a few years shy. The teen pregnant when Slow Bear intercepted them, an unwelcome bonus after he beat the shit out of their driver. Broke his jaw. The only reason he didn't break more at the time was to avoid adding another murder to his conscience. They'd been piling up fast.

He killed the same sick fuck later, though. He should've saved himself the time. His conscience had given him the thumbs up.

Slow Bear caught himself falling asleep. Then he dreamed he woke up and drove away…shit, where would he go? The rez didn't want him, and most likely believed he was dead anyway, since it was what he wanted them to believe.

Or Williston, North Dakota, again? A one-armed Indian begging for work on the dying oil patch?

Or Nebraska? His dream carried him across the country, a little subdivision on the edge of soybean fields outside the town of Worms. A safe place for the girls with a one-night stand who turned into something more. Or at least, something else.

Abeline. Sixty-years-old and fucked like a woman who'd been fucking for at least forty-four years.

In the dream, she opened the door for him wearing a cowboy hat and not much else. The girls – Pia and Melody – happy and clean and smiling bright. Pia in braces, making it to the dentist for the first time in her life. They had school books and juice boxes and Skittles, like any girls their age should.

A car horn in the distance woke him. Slow Bear jolted, imagining he'd been caught. But no, nobdy around. Just Shitfoot swirling, swirling, swirling. The water was starting to stink.

Had Pia and Melody been delivered to his front door, the service he'd paid dearly for, he would've let them play with the toys and given them cake and ice cream and let them swim in the pool, and when it was time for them to take a bath before bed…

Slow Bear wished he had the strength to pick up the meat cleaver and keep wailing on him.

The pedo had made his money in the movie business. Not by

acting or directing or producing or writing. He made his money by renting the lights, the rigs, the cameras, the lenses and filters, the editing equipment, all digital now, microphones and headsets and nearly every other little thing necessary on a movie set the directors and actors all took for granted. His son helped run the family business, which also meant handling his father's expensive tastes. As long as Shitfoot Junior didn't have to actually *see* any of it, all he was doing was making calls. Making arrangements. Could've been anything, really, like a set of director's chairs for a *Jurassic Park* sequel.

The pedo's daughter was in on it, too. But she wouldn't show up until Daddy gave her the "all clear," via text, saying he was done with the girls. Then it was her turn to…

Euphemism for "send them on down the food chain."

He shuddered.

Like some disgusting pedo pecking order? An ePerv auction site?

Or a quick shot of something to make the girls sleepy, slip them into the Pacific somewhere?

Maybe Slow Bear should text her the all clear from her daddy's phone and wait for her, meat mallet in hand.

A fine idea.

Wait, where was the mallet?

Dropped it in the goddamned pool.

So tired.

God, yes, he needed to sleep. Maybe dream a little more about his surrogate family in Nebraska. He ought to send Abeline a postcard.

Another sniff and grimace at the pool. Should he clean up before heading inside? The privacy fence was tall enough and the neighbors far enough away, Slow Bear thought, *fuck it.* Instead, he stumbled around until he found the pool supplies and dumped all the bleach into the nasty thing. The pig blood water went pink. The fumes nearly choked him, which he absolutely didn't need. He crawled as far away as he could, into the grass between house and fake-tropical paradise, and puked until he was dry.

Only then did he crawl the rest of the way inside, find the nearest bed with too many pillows and stuffed animals, and black out before he could lift his legs onto the mattress.

Chapter 2

The fog in his head was slowly dissipating. Slow Bear had forgotten how he'd made it to California from Salt Lake City.

He thought he'd died in a smoke-filled basement, sick with Covid, but the next thing he knew, he was laying on the grass outside, a swarm of firemen and a couple cops standing over him, shouting "ARE YOU OKAY?" even as they fought to slip an air mask over his head so he wouldn't be able to answer anyway.

AREYOUOKAYAREYOUOKAYAREYOUOKAY?

He picked up chatter, cop chatter: "Bloodbath in the dining room."

"He good for it?"

"For what? What the fuck happened in here?"

He picked up neighbor chatter, talking about the former owner: "I told you something was off about him."

"I always thought he was queer."

"Naw, man, queers are alright. I think he was an antifa."

Ambulance came along. If he'd had his way, Slow Bear would've sent his spirit floating beyond his body and the pain, the burns, the struggle to breath, drowning on dry land. Watch from above himself in perfect peace as he arose into the afterlife.

This ain't that.

Every jolt was juiced up to eleven. Yeah, like Nigel Tufnel. *Eh-leh-vhen.*

They lifted his ass – his *whole* ass – onto the gurney. "Ow, ow, ow, fuck," he said into the mask. Nobody listened.

A cop cuffed Slow Bear's wrist to the gurney while the EMTs tried to stop him, a white boy from central casting and a black woman who must've been a wrestler in her younger days.

"Uhn-uh, we don't need shackles right now!"

"He's under arrest! You want me to arrest you, too?"

"Get the fuck away from me so I can do my job. He dies, it's on you!"

"My hands are clean, my hands are *clean!*"

They slid Slow Bear into of the ambulance and slammed the doors, jolting his neck and back and knees and head. The bracelet rattled and stung on his wrist.

Alive or teetering, he couldn't decide. He was fine with giving up the ghost. All he had to do was will himself to fly away, sweet Lord.

Not so easy. His body *yearned* to live, the bastard. Breathing was harder than it had ever been. He had to force himself to keep it up, sure he'd die if he left it up to his *medulla oblongata.* How in the deepest fuck did he remember what a *medulla oblongata* was? Sounds like a Police album.

Cops and EMTs outside the van sounded like they were revving up for a battle royal. Then the doors flew open, and the woman climbed in cursing under her breath, followed by a Bubba-looking cop – weren't they all?

"S'all right, baby, you still with me?"

Then she injected him with a shot of oblivion.

Chapter 3

Slow Bear woke again when his top half slid off the bed he'd failed to climb into at Shitfoot's mansion. Also because Shitfoot's phone was buzzing up a storm. Good thing he'd forced the pedo to thumbprint it to life.

The name on the screen was Lulu Doll. The photo beneath her name, a smiling wind-blown brunette in sunglasses and candy apple red lipstick, matched up to the couple pics of Shitfoot's daughter he'd seen. He was terrible at ages. Twenty? Forty?

He let the call go to voice mail while he pushed himself off the floor and slumped against the bed. Much darker out now. How long had he been asleep? Checked the phone time – eight-twenty-one PM – but couldn't remember what time he'd killed the kiddie-rapist or how long he sat by the pool and watched the man drift or what "time" was anyway, in a conceptual, existential sense, but it was dark now. He was starving. The phone buzzed again. She'd left a message.

First, he should get on his feet.

Five full minutes later…

He used the wall as a crutch and flipped on light switches along the way to the kitchen. A massive fucking kitchen. The sort of kitchen you'd feel embarrassed eating a Pop Tart in. The sort of kitchen designed to keep guys like him *out*. The island alone as big as the bedroom. At first, Slow Bear didn't think there was a fridge or dishwasher because they were covered in wood.

He found the fridge, but no orange juice, the only drink helping keep the Big Bad Heroin away. Lost one addiction only to replace it with a more expensive one – you'd think oranges were made of gold. Instead, plenty of juice boxes, Gogurt, apple slices, ugh. In the freezer, frozen pizza rolls, egg rolls, and ice cream cartons packed full, almost spilling off the shelves when he opened the door.

Dairy on his stomach right now? No thanks. He tossed the egg rolls into the microwave. Five minutes.

He kept foraging.

A whole line of sugary cereals. Rabbits and Frankenberries and Cap'n and Krispies.

Jackpot.

Slow Bear took the Cap'n, peanut butter if he remembered from long ago. Flipped the box. It said so right on the front. A bit delirious, he shoved his hand into the box, grabbed a handful of the stuff, and forgot he didn't have another hand to hold the box. First time in a long time. The box tumbled, puked its insides all over the floor before landing flat.

He shoved most of his handful in his mouth and checked his other options. Honey Smacks sounded fine.

While he sat at the island on a mid-century modern stool, uncomfortable as a stick up the ass, and ate Honey Smacks with egg rolls, he listened to the message on Shitfoot's phone.

Lulu Doll, eh? Weird to call your daughter "doll" but it was the least weird thing Slow Bear had seen about these people, these fucking traffickers and kiddie-rapists, fucking kidnappers, like the ones who'd taken his friend, Lady.

Lady Bartender, the way he thought of her, even though her name was Kylie. The whole reason Slow Bear had salted the motherfucking earth between the rez in North Dakota and Shitfoot's hill in San Bernadino was hunting for Lady. Instead he rescued the creep's package, nearly died (again), and killed only a tiny fraction of the assholes involved in this maddeningly lucrative horseshit.

"Daddy? Hello? Daddy?" Lulu Doll sure put on a Chatty Cathy porn voice. "You'd better not have let your phone die on your play date. Call me soon as you get this, but I'm coming over. I've heard some things, bad things, coming out of Utah. We need to get rid of, um, I'll tell you when we talk. I'm ten minutes away, and I don't want to *see* your playmates, understand? Daddy?"

Beep.

Slow Bear scrolled through the missed calls. She'd been trying for the last hour, six, seven times and left her voice mail eleven minutes ago.

Eleven minutes.

I'm ten minutes away.

A key rattled in the front door lock, around the corner and out of view in the open concept first floor. House alarm chirped, then four more chirps, the code typed in.

"Daddy! Daddy! Answer your phone, daddy! You'd better be decent."

High heels clicked across the tile.

By the time she rounded the corner, Slow Bear was already across the island to the drawers and hoped he'd find a knife.

Instead, he found a ladle. A metal ladle, at least.

Lulu Doll stopped and looked at the Cap'n Crunch mess all over the floor, then the Honey Smacks now scattered everywhere, then to Slow Bear holding a fucking ladle.

"Jesus!"

He threw the ladle at her.

It was a heavy ladle, he'd give it credit. Hit her square on the mouth. Blood burst from her lip and Slow Bear swore he saw a tooth fly.

It gave him time to rifle around for a two-pronged serving fork.

Lulu had fallen right off her heels, down like a sack of potatoes, the Lubatoons or Jimmy Choo-Choos not doing her favors. Her ankle buckled. She spit a shrill "*Shit!*"

Slow Bear rounded the island and stood over her with the fork while she caught her breath and dribbled blood and spit.

He could not deny she was a spicy number. Hair styled up, must have cost a grand. The shoes must've cost even more, but might as well be bear traps for all the good they'd done. Bony legs, shiny from moisturizer. She wore the type of short skirt-suit that told the world, "My business is sex and business is good."

She smeared blood across her cheek with the back of her hand.

"Look what you've done! You piece of shit, what were you thinking?"

Then a high lonesome whine:

"*Daaaddyyyyy*. What have I told you about letting other people play with your toys? What have I told you?"

She scrambled to her feet, more like a long-legged spider trying to find footing in a big wind. Winced putting weight on her heels, but slipped the straps off and let them drop to the floor. Tried her foot again. Flat long feet with angry corns, but otherwise suckable toes, Slow Bear thought. She limped a step or two, then seemed fine.

She wagged a finger at him, tongue punching around inside her mouth. "You owe me a fucking tooth. Wait here."

As she disappeared into the hallway, heading to the room where Slow Bear had dozed, most likely, he stood thinking, *Why am I listening to her?*

He followed her.

She babbled the whole time. "You have *got* to be *more careful*, Daddy, I keep telling you, and Darwin keeps telling you, and Pamela keeps telling you. Some things money won't help. You won't *believe* what I heard out of Utah. Wild story, *wild*. We need to hurry and get ahead of –"

Stopped. Dead.

She stepped out of the bedroom, holding on to the doorframe. Crinkles around her eyes. Slow Bear standing there, fork at his side.

She counted his arms. His arm.

"Have you…have you seen my father?"

Slow Bear waved the fork towards the backyard. "Try the pool."

She blinked, nodded, then stalked past him, a little more tense.

He let her slide the glass door open before trailing. Asking himself, *Why? Why are you letting her wander around free? Why aren't you putting the fear of God into her?*

Ain't much God had done to Slow Bear could stop him doing what he was doing. Didn't seem The Big Dick would phase Lulu Doll either.

Especially since she'd surely found her daddy by then and wasn't screaming at the top of her tanned, fit, and obviously bottomless lungs.

Slow Bear stepped out onto the patio. Lulu Doll stood at the edge of the pool, the lights underwater glowing now, her feet in a puddle of blood and bleach. Staring at her dad's body, still swirling in clouds of red and gray, the bleach working overtime.

At least the fumes had dissipated. Still, Slow Bear coughed, cleared his throat.

Lulu turned, her lip still bleeding. Blank.

What could he say? He shrugged.

"The one-armed Indian?"

"Yeah."

"From Utah?"

Another shrug. Shruggy McShrugerton. "I mean, North Dakota, originally."

"You…you killed…everybody."

"Don't give me too much credit. Maybe half everybody." Gravity was fucking with him again. He lowered himself into a chair at the poolside table, tossed his fork on top. He held his head up with his hand. "Take a seat."

"Um. No."

"Suit yourself."

"You're going to kill me, too."

"Mm hm."

Chapter 4

Oblivion didn't help much.

His whole body wracked with lightning as the gurney wheels dropped and smacked the ground about the same time some motherfucker shouted "No way! No! Put him back. Not here."

His EMT guardian angel shouted, "This a hospital, isn't it? You still treat sick people?"

"You've got eyes. See the crowd in the ER? We're running out of beds."

"Take the gurney. Put him in the hall. He needs help!"

"Can't do it. Won't do it. Find somewhere else that takes pedophiles."

"Excuse me?"

Slow Bear opened his eyes, expected to find someone pouring acid into them, but no such luck. At least acid would've explained the pain.

The shouting ER nurse was a fat white man with a pointy beard and waxed mustache in baby-blue scrubs. No surgical mask, inches from his EMT's face. Fogged up her face shield.

"He's from the fire? I heard it was a pedophile's house, full of sick motherfuckers. Do yourself a favor and dump him in the desert."

"Man, you're serious? What about do no harm? What about Jesus saying the least of these?"

He stepped back, hands up. "Not here. We're a Catholic hospital. Old Testament wrath, far as I give a shit."

He turned for the glass doors when another ambulance screamed up and the driver slammed it into park and got out shouting, "Covid! I got Covid here! Got Covid!"

Slow Bear thought, *So do I, but you don't hear me bitching about it.*

The beardy nurse had no problem STAT-ing the shit out of him, everyone doing their best Clooney to get the old man inside, knowing he was a lost cause.

The lady EMT with the rock hard muscles and face reminding Slow Bear of a goddess sculpture shouted, "Lord, lord, Jesus." To her driver and the Bubba cop, "Someone's got to take him."

"You heard the man," the cop said, unclipping his holster. "Give me the word and he's not our problem anymore."

She peered down at Slow Bear. "Damn, boy. Don't have a friend in the world, do you?"

He was about to wave her closer, but found they'd chained his fucking hand anyway. Chinned her closer, then.

She squatted beside the gurney. "Say what?"

"Not a pedophile," he said. It barely qualified as speech. "Not a pedophile. Killed them all."

The cop leaned in, made a face at the smell – smoke and puke and Bear stank. "Jesus. He confessing?"

"Shut up, will you? Say again, hon?"

"Saved the girls. Killed the motherfuuu…" Dizzy.

The EMT was tall. "Said he's not one of the sickos. Said he's going to *die* if we don't get him help, then we'll never know the full story."

"Shit." The driver, masked-up, muffled. "How far's the next hospital?"

"Not worth the drive if they won't take him either. Why don't you call ahead and see? Find someone else to help other than Beefy the Beard, please."

The driver set off on his chore. The EMT lady had what it took, you know? Leadership, persuasion, whatever it was.

Turned to Slow Bear. "No joke? You saved some girls?"

Slow Bear held up two fingers. "Two."

"If I find out you're lying –"

"Honest injun."

"Mister…" Flicked her eyes at the cop again. "Hey, Bubba, help me lift him into the van again."

"Bubba, sister? Call me Officer, how bout?"

"You gonna help?"

He bitched and moaned but he did it.

Twice as jolted, Slow Bear was now fully awake and wheezing through soot *and* Covid, wondering what in the mighty fuck he'd done to piss off Jesus, his ancestors, the Great Spirit, Mother Nature, and Santa Claus so bad they wouldn't let his raggedy ass die already.

"Thank you, officer, I appreciate your help."

"Tell you what. Sit up front next time and I'll see to it he takes his medicine. I promise, no gun."

Slow Bear almost shouted, *Yes, please, I'll take it*, but couldn't make the effort.

They were out of his sightline, Slow Bear lying in the ambulance, wishing he had his hand free to grope for an oxygen mask. Every breath promising a better next one, every next breath breaking the promise.

The EMT sighed. "Maybe so. I don't know. Let's wait until Wayne gets back, see what the Lutherans say. Think you could get us both a coffee?"

"What if I stay with the prisoner and you go get the coffee?"

"Patient, not prisoner. Patient. And he's a patient first until they tell us he's not anymore. I ain't going nowhere. I like lots of cream and Splenda."

"Alright. It's waiting room coffee, you know. I'm not walking to Starbucks."

"Fine, fine. As long as it's caffeinated."

He set off, Slow Bear heard the footsteps. Soon as they faded, though, the ambulance doors *throomed* shut.

Driver's door opened, slammed, then the engine roared and they bolted forward, the gurney not locked in, bouncing left and right, swinging, banging, Slow Bear white knuckleing the damned thing.

Then he grinned.

Crazy bitch kidnapped him.

Chapter 5

Lulu Doll shook her head and drifted over to the table. Sat across from him. Slow Bear wasn't sure she knew she was doing it. "Emmy was a friend of mine." Hugged herself good and hard.

"Who?"

"Emmy. Her name was Imelda."

"Sorry, doesn't help."

"Imelda! You fucking shot her in Carl's Jr."

"Which one?"

"You shot her face off."

Widened his eyes. "Oh, her. I thought she was the other one. I didn't shoot her."

"Not what I heard."

"I couldn't have shot her. They took my gun from me. It was Petey."

Not a pretty scene, he remembered. Meeting the couriers looking to exchange the girls – Pia and Melody – for the next part of their trip out west, which was MT's house in Utah where Slow Bear thought he'd died. But he could've died in Carl's Jr. in Denver, too. He wasn't good at strategizing.

He'd pieced together there were a lot of upper-class traffickers all over these United States with no goddamn souls willing to trade kids or working-class Native or immigrant girls for a fat and tall pile of money.

He chinned towards the pool. "No tears for dear ol' daddy?"

A deep sigh. "I'm in shock."

"The fuck you are."

"Please. I've snorted too much blow today. The only way I can deal with his…fuck. His play dates." She laughed, but it wasn't happy. "His play dates. Did you catch him in the act, then? Today's playmates?"

"Someone rang the doorbell. I let it go." Slow Bear shuddered. "Calling them 'playmates'. I should've…he was far enough gone by then, I could've saved…shit."

"They'd keep coming. If my father doesn't answer his door, we had a Plan B for those girls, rest assured."

His heart plunged straight to his guts. Thinking about Pia. Thinking about Melody. Thinking about Shitfoot opening his door to them, sick smile and a barely tied bathrobe, same as when Slow Bear rang the bell earlier in the day.

"By the way," she said, two fingers out on the table top, should be a cigarette between them. Probably was most of any other day. "Where are the girls you took from Gerardo?"

"Safe."

"Better hope so. But, hey, you did it. Saved two. Two of, let's see, infinity." She gave him a golf clap.

He searched the ground. What had he done with the meat mallet? Remembered again – bottom of the pool.

Lulu Doll's coked-up grin faded. The fake clap faded. She shrunk, feet turned in. Reminded him a little of Pia for a moment.

Her hand darted across to the fork. She held it up between them. Nostrils flaring.

"What you said earlier, on the phone? About what I did in Utah?"

"Please."

"You think a fork is going to help you?" He let her think about it. "Listen, I don't mind us talking and all, but you being with these motherfuckers who wanted to send my two favorite *children* into your daddy's house of horror, well, I don't look kindly on it. So tell me when you're ready to go. I'll make it quick and painless, a deal I did not offer your daddy."

Slow Bear expected crying, pleading, or for her to make a mad dash for the house. She did none of it. A moment of silence stretched to a minute, more. Choosing how she wanted to die. *Pills*, he thought. *She'd probably choose pills*. Meaning he'd have to babysit her ass most of the night to make sure it actually worked. Instead, he could try to sell her on a bottle of sleeping pills, a warm bath, and a sharp blade.

"I was his first, you know."

"What?"

"Daddy. Daddy's first." She dropped the fork to her lap. "I was fourteen. Lucky, I guess, he hadn't lowered his eyes yet. Know what I mean? I looked older than my age, developed faster. I was easy pickings."

"Where was your mom?"

Her laugh was the most bitter sound he'd heard in years. "When she wasn't off fucking his friends, she was right beside me, jealous as shit. They started out swingers, see? But then…yeah, threesomes with my parents. I am not fucking lying. All her plastic surgery, her gym time, all because of me. Who could I tell? Who the fuck could I tell?"

He wondered, still, if she'd told anyone. How much had she been holding in, now ready to vomit up for Slow Bear?

How much of it was even true, not utter horseshit?

No clue who to believe anymore. Just the girls. Believe the girls.

Even this girl?

"You told someone, though."

Itched her nose. Sniffed. "My stepbrother, I didn't know him well. We're a decade apart. He'd already graduated college. Real close with my mom – a bit freakishly close, if you ask me – but always a bit standoffish with Dad, not his real dad anyway. He picked up on it, though, the way Daddy hugged me, kissed me, not the way a dad should, you know?"

Bubbles in the pool around Shitfoot. Gas building, escaping the body. Lulu Doll hugged herself again, arms on her knees.

"You sure you want to talk about it?"

"Fine, it's fine. Not like it helps, sure doesn't hurt. Yeah, my stepbrother, Darwin, he caught on, asked me about it. He *listened.* He asked if I wanted it to stop. Of course I did! Fuck's sake, my own father." Another sniff. "Darwin was the only one I could trust, it seemed. He cared."

"I know where this is going."

"Jesus, rude."

"Told you we didn't have to talk about it."

"My stepbrother seduced me. Yes. I fucked him. A lot. Oh god, a whole lot. I thought we were in love. We were. It really was love. But it was, you know, complicated. Took me a long time to see it. How he used me."

"Used?"

"It was one thing for him to stand up to Dad, which he did. But that wasn't what did it. I was getting older and he was getting bored. Darwin started planting the seeds. Found him another teenage playmate. Then a younger playmate."

"Stop calling them playmates."

"I mean, it's what we call them, okay? It just is."

"Your brother found a way to get your dad hooked on younger girls."

She tapped her cigarette fingers on the table. Dying for a smoke.

"It's not like he was *forced* or anything. All Darwin had to do was present the opportunity, and Dad lapped it up. Maybe once, *maybe*, he held back a minute, asked Darwin if they should stop. If it was wrong. Can you believe it? The man had to *ask* if it was wrong. He knew it was wrong. He didn't want to stop. He wanted *permission*."

"Darwin gave it to him."

"Fuck yes, Darwin gave it to him. Did he ever. The whole time, Darwin was recording. Hours and hours and Dad and the playmates, the girls. Blackmail if he ever needed leverage."

Lulu Doll rolled her eyes. "Meanwhile, Mom's on the party scene. Orgies. Heroin. Darwin kept her in a state of bliss. Soon as Dad was done with me, he was done with her, too. She wanted a divorce. Wanted to take his pedophile ass to the cleaners. But it was Darwin who told her there was a better way. A more satisfying way."

"A more lucrative way."

"Now you're catching on. First, he told Dad about the tapes, showed him a sample. Then, he showed a tape of *me*. Not sex, no, lucky me. Darwin made one of me giving a deposition. A fake one. It was pretty cool."

"About him?"

"Yes, and Darwin paid Dad's own lawyer to be in on it. He was seriously fucked. Unless…"

"He let Darwin handle everything."

"*Ev-ree-thing.* The business, the finances, the investments, the cash, the lawyers, all of it. And he would keep getting Dad new playmates, new girls, I mean, girls. Victims."

The funny thing, to Slow Bear, anyway, was how Lulu Doll thought she was psychoanalyzing her way out of dying. A California quirk, probably.

She had no idea.

"So…why are you helping? If you're out, why are you here doing his dirty work."

"Oh, come on. It's not like I have a choice."

"Sure you do."

"No, I don't. I really don't. Because once Darwin showed Daddy my tape, he deleted it. Poof. Gone. But you want to know why Darwin's a genius, it's shit like this. Listen." Holding court, like at a club with her pals drinking Gin Rickeys. "The deposition was long. He told me it had to feel real. I think he told the other lawyers – actors, I think – we were rehearsing for a movie. Screen test. After he deleted the first one, he showed me another one he'd edited to sound like I was full of shit. Same seven hours, edited, but with different questions, I kept contradicting myself, like I'd baited him, led him on. My own dad."

His heart, the one that'd fallen into his guts? It wanted out through his throat now. He was exhausted, sickened, pissed, sad, and wishing he could hear Abeline's cornpone voice tell him the girls were okay.

"He's blackmailing you, too."

"Not, like, blackmail so much as, you know, I don't have a better option."

"You're wearing designer clothes, living the high life as far as I can surmise. Got good money. How old are you now?"

Lulu Doll sucked in her cheeks. "Twenty-six."

No way. "So, twelve years in the biz."

"Uh, *no*. Jesus. You know, I finished high school. I went to college. Summa cum laude, even. Public relations."

"Then, back to my question."

She leaned across the table, eye to eye. "Darwin pays me a fuck-ton of money to arrange the transportation, talk with brokers, handle translators –"

Say what?

"Hold up, wait, wait. He's making enough money from your dad's equipment rental racket to cover it?"

Lulu Doll stutter-hissed, "S-s-s-see, no no no, it's not…I thought you knew."

"I don't get it."

"Like, you thought my dad was trafficking."

"I thought your dad tried to buy those girls."

"Yeah, he did, he does. It's like retail versus wholesale. Or, or, or, free samples?"

Almost worth diving into the bloody bool for the meat mallet.

Lulu Doll kept on, "My dad, he's barely aware, *was*, was barely aware of what was going on outside his house anymore. Darwin kept him drunk, sent the girls regularly, He was reduced to an animal. Urges, needs. Even worse was when he got really bored, he started inviting over other pervs, people in Hollywood, executives, actors. I thought you were one of those for a moment, the more the merrier, my dad thought."

"You said 'free samples.' How was he getting free samples?"

Her breathing tightened, her voice wavered. "Darwin. Once he figured out, you know, the *business*, their business, the movers, the *traffickers*, and cut better deals. Before long, he had taken over some of the operations, consolidated them. Muscled others out. Child Sex Limited, you know? Didn't you know?"

Slow Bear swallowed but his mouth was bone dry. He coughed, hacked, still nowhere near well. "Darwin. Your brother. He's the wizard? It's all his business?"

"One of them. One of the biggest. He washes the money through his winery, up in Paso Robles. It's his passion. It's good stuff, high quality. Paid for by sex slaves."

"Fuck." He stood. "*Fuck!*"

"He never touches the girls. No kids. After me, I don't know what he did. He's single, maybe bi? Maybe a monk? Or maybe, ugh, maybe with my own mom?"

"Jesus, enough."

"He pays her. More than he pays me. He bought her a retreat outside Sedona, like a wellness spa. She pretends to be a holistic guru even though she shoots smack, fucks like a rabbit, and binges pasta, purges. Gross."

"Shut up, would you? Shut the fuck up!"

Slow Bear was done. He didn't want to hear any more. Whatever traces of Covid were left in his blood landed a haymaker. He stumbled, almost took a header into the pool, but fell on the concrete inches away, his bad shoulder taking the impact.

Lulu Doll came to him, instinct, it seemed, but then must've remembered he was no friend, kept her distance. He fell onto his back, heaved breaths.

The girl frittered and paced. "Shit. Shit. I shouldn't have told you. Shit. I need to call Darwin. He can smooth it over, don't worry. He can set you up, pay you for your trouble, how about? You don't have to hurt me. You don't. You killing Dad saved us all a headache and a lot of money. You've done us a favor."

Is this why she hadn't run? Was she more worried about how Darwin would react than to Slow Bear murdering her?

Darwin. The fucker "evolved" into a trafficking kingpin. Should've been him in the bathrobe floating in the pool. Should be all three of them. Four if you count the mother.

Free Samples.

Playmates.

Child Sex Limited.

But wait.

"Hey, come here." He waved her over. Held out his hand. "Help me sit."

She didn't. She kept frittering. "I bet I don't even have to call. I can wire it into your account. Or Venmo? I can Venmo it."

"Do I look like I Venmo? Help me up, I said."

She did. Took his hand, helped him sit.

"Listen," he said, still coughing. "Your brother. I need to talk to him."

"Let me get my phone. You can call."

"No, no, I mean, in person."

"I don't get why –"

"I think he can help me find a friend I lost."

The stench from the pool didn't help. He rolled to his knees and started crawling away.

"But first, I need a fucking shower."

Chapter 6

When the EMT finally jolted to a stop, Slow Bear, shrunk into a fetal pose, was grateful. Still couldn't figure out why she'd taken him, though. Not like they couldn't track her ambulance these days. Right?

The rear doors opened and the sunlight struck him down, blind like Saul on the road to Damascus. He blinked back until his eyes cleared.

She climbed into the ambulance. "Sorry about the drive."

"Fuck sake." He rattled the handcuff against the bed railing. "Forget something?"

"It was spur of the moment. I'm sorry, okay? Hold on."

She shuffled through the supplies and machines and broken vials and bandages, bandages, bandages *everywhere*. She found a red plastic first aid kit – wasn't the whole ambulance a rolling first aid kit? – and rifled through it, brought out a pair of wire cutters.

"Seriously?"

"You have no idea the weird shit we've seen. You add new tools every week."

She wedged the cutters between his skin and the steel ring. Took a lot of effort, grunting, but she finally got it. Hurt pretty bad, too, but Slow Bear gritted his teeth and, hey, it wasn't broken. All peachy.

She helped him out. They were in a neighborhood. An average run-down neighborhood. Not run-down trashy, but showing its age. Single-family homes, lot of stucco, close together, wooden fences separating every postage stamp backyard. They were parked in a driveway, a mint green home, a front yard worn to dirt and a few clumps of grass, not long for this world. In front of the ambulance was a silver Cadillac CTS, had to be twenty years old, under a simple aluminum carport, one leg bent in. You'd have to duck under to get in the passenger door.

His head still swimmy, Slow Bear followed the EMT to the side door. But why? It had only been forty-five minutes since he'd been found in the basement, dragged upstairs and dumped on the lawn before the ambulance sped him away. He didn't know her name, she'd kidnapped him, and the cop had said killing Slow Bear would take a whole lot of shit off everyone's plates. Wouldn't be the first ambush he'd blithely walked into.

Another thing, it didn't hit him until just then, no cops around, no one sticking needles in him, trying to fit oxygen masks on him, handcuffing him, finally: *Did Abeline and the girls make it home?* He was afraid to call and find out. The traffickers had the whole U S of A wired.

"Wait, wait a sec." He limped to the side of the driveway and choked up a thin stream of black bile. He wiped his mouth and nodded. Good to go.

The EMT turned the knob and knocked at the same time. "It's me, Mama."

A shout from the other room, "Me who?"

"Me, Mama. Toni."

Checked off one item.

"Your house?" Slow Bear followed her into a small kitchen, squeaky linoleum and forty-year-old appliances, too many colors clashing.

"Mama's house. I ain't taking the ambulance to my own house. They track us, you know."

"They're tracking us right now? Jesus, you'll lead them straight to us."

She gave Slow Bear a look, you know the look, like, *I'm smarter than you.*

"I'll tell them my mama had an emergency. She fell! Nobody else to help her."

"Still –"

"Mama, need you to give me a hand."

They walked through to the living room, more modern than the kitchen. Puffy couches and end-chairs, huge TV, and a recliner that might as well've been a throne. Sitting in it was an older black woman, much smaller than her daughter. Lighter skin tone, too. Ankles crossed and hands overlapping on her chest. Bright pink sweatpants and a silk blouse a woman might wear to a business meeting. Nary a wrinkle, except around her mouth. Slow Bear did the math and thought if she's in her late sixties now, she's going to live to a hundred and fifteen.

"You going to introduce me to your friend?"

Toni *hm*-ed and *um*-ed. Turned her head. "What's your name?"

"Micah." He tipped a hat he wasn't wearing. "Hi, I'm Micah."

"Yes, Micah, my mother. Mama, he's –"

"A one-armed man who smells like a tire fire. Good lord, son, what have you gotten yourself into?"

"Out of, really. A burning house."

"Mm." Cut her eyes at Toni. "For real?"

"Mama, I need you to drive him over to Cheetah's apartment, okay? Right away. Let him get cleaned up, take a nap. Maybe cook him a good supper."

"At Cheetah's? You think the food ain't spoiled?"

"I don't know, Mama." She planted her hands on her hips. "I'm in a hurry, though. This is important."

Mama turned to her TV. Otherwise, hadn't moved a muscle. "Why can't he stay here? Or at your house? I mean, young man, Micah, the bath's through there if you want a shower." She waved towards a hallway leading out of the living room towards the rest of the house.

"Mama, it's a Jesus thing, okay?"

It amused the old lady. She smirked. "A Jesus thing?"

"Yes, a Jesus thing, no questions asked."

Mama shook her head against the plush cushion of her recliner. Comfortable. Slow Bear wanted to sit down, drifted towards the couch without thinking about it and was inches from the seat when –

"No, no, I'm not having him sitting on my clean couch. Not looking like a chimney sweep. No sir. You get your ass up."

Slow Bear caught himself, but fell to the impossibly clean beige carpet, leaving a soot stain.

"Lord have mercy." Mama declined her footrest with a pop and a clang, stood up from the chair. "Hope you know how to steam clean a carpet."

"Mama, when I say I don't have time, I mean it. I promise, I'll explain later."

Toni reached for Slow Bear's arm and helped him up. Woozy, tiny atomic explosions behind his eyes when he shifted them. Another hard cough coming on.

Held it…

Until he couldn't.

Mama leapt like she'd been tazed. "Does he have Covid? Did you bring Covid into my home? Waltzed Covid on up into my house?"

"No, Mama."

"Yes, Mama." Slow Bear finding voice in his ripped-to-shreds throat. "Sorry, I'm real sorry."

"Get him out. Get his ass out of my house. Lord, Toni, what were you thinking?"

"I didn't know!"

"How can you not…Toni!" Mama on the verge of tears.

Toni reached for her mom, who pulled away, but got her on the next try. Held her by outstretched arms. "I didn't know. But it's going to be okay. It's a Jesus thing, and Jesus things are good, remember? Please? Don't make me beg. If I take him with me now, someone's going to kill him."

Mama let out a deep breath, lips quivering, but her eyes, burning rage. Slow Bear wasn't sure he wanted to be anywhere with her, let alone some place where a cheetah lives.

The rage burned itself out. Squeezed down like coal into a diamond.

Mama squeezed her daughter's arms. "I'll get my keys."

"Thank you, Mama."

"Go on, get out of here. Go."

Toni started to leave. "She'll take good care of you, and I'll see you later."

Slow Bear didn't know what to say. Still didn't know what was going on, who these people were, and why he should trust them. He went with, "I owe you one."

She grinned and was gone.

Mama started for the hallway to her bedroom. "Back in a minute. Don't even think of sitting on anything. In fact, wait in the kitchen. Don't sit down in there, neither."

Fine, he thought. He wobbled into the kitchen and sat his ass in one of her old space-age yellow-vinyl kitchen chairs anyway.

Chapter 7

Slow Bear dragged Lulu Doll from room to room in the mansion. She was still more concerned with what her stepbrother might think than what Slow Bear had threatened to do to her.

Warbling away, if only to hear the sound of her own voice. Maybe it calmed her down. "Not to be presumptuous, but if you need help showering, I don't mind. I really don't. I can climb in with you. Or, how about, Daddy has a Jacuzzi in his en suite, big enough for both of us. Feel real good, I bet."

"I don't need help."

"It doesn't have to be *help*, then, if you want to, like, relax, you know. Set Darwin off to the side for now and have fun, right? God, you could use some."

"Some what?"

A giggle. "Some *fun*, some *some*, like get some, want some. Me and you."

He stopped dead in his tracks. Lulu Doll ran into him. He turned, peered down.

"Me and you?"

A skittery smile. "Yeah, come on. Let's turn on the Jacuzzi and soak. Follow me."

She ran her left foot up her right calf.

He shook his head and dragged her along, searching room to room. "You're not my type."

"I'm fucking adorable, what do you mean I'm not your type?"

"I like older women."

He finally found what he needed in a game room, a big TV up on the wall with a Playstation and nearly a hundred games lined up in a media case, old-school consoles, pinball machines, a mini-basketball game. Who was this room for? Had Shitfoot gotten into boys, too? Slow Bear didn't want to know. He dropped Lulu Doll's arm and reached behind the TV and media stand, grabbed a bunch of cables and ripped them out – the TV anchored well, but the Playstation flying, cracking into the screen, instant spider-web.

"Whoa, watch it! The fuck, man?"

Slow Bear freed the wires – HDMI and RCA and power cords – and left the room. "Where's the shower? Closest one will do."

Lulu Doll pointed him a short way down the hall to a bathroom with a tub/shower combo, sparkly shower curtain, plenty of fluffy towels on a rack beside the tub, and a lot of gels and scrubs and shampoos and conditioners, pinks and greens and purples.

"You sure you don't need help?"

He waved her in. "How about you lay face down on the floor for me?"

"Okay. But what if…?" She unbuttoned the top two buttons on her blouse. "Help me with the rest?"

Slow Bear dropped his cables, took Lulu Doll by the wrist, and forced her to her knees, then down to her stomach. He eased his knee firmly into the small of her back, not enough to hurt, then surprised himself by hog-tying the girl pretty well with only one-hand.

She kicked and shouted once he'd bound her hands, but he finally used his weight and leverage to get her ankles bound, a gold HDMI cable tethering them.

She kept fighting, but the knots looked secure. "Piece of shit! Goddamn it, I was *nice* to you! Motherfucker! I swear, you won't get anywhere near Darwin if you don't untie me *right now*. Right *now*!"

He ignored her, tossed a few bottles of bath gel into the tub and started the water. Wanted a good long hot one.

"I was trying to *help* you!"

He kicked off his boots, unbuttoned his shirt, let it fall to the floor. Then his belt. Stopped. Glanced down. Murder on Lulu

Doll's face. "You mind closing your eyes? Turning away?"

"Are you fucking serious?"

"Do it, alright? Before I tie a bag on your head or something."

She made horse snorts but turned her head away from Slow Bear, cheek on the cold tile.

Slow Bear dropped his jeans and jockeys and stepped on the toes of his socks to pull them off. The shower was good and steamy, the mirror fogged, vapor swirling around him. He eased into the shower, winced when the hot needles stung his skin.

Glory be! As Mama might've said.

The shower felt almost as good as his first at Cheetah's apartment, when he'd sat in the tub and let the shower rain down on him, arm around his knees, still processing what had happened at the house of horrors in Salt Lake City. All the chaos, all the violence, all his fault, it didn't feel like *him* doing it. Except it did, like, the pain of it, the strain. But actually doing it, killing the sick fucks, like used car dealers for sex slaves. A Hulk moment. Possession. Angel of Death shit.

He'd choked back tears sitting in Cheetah's tub until he couldn't anymore and let it out in howls loud enough for Mama to come running. "Jesus, boy, shush now! What's wrong? What happened?"

He told her it was okay, a few aches and pains.

Those were nothing compared to him being alive at all. The only reason he sent Abeline and the girls away was because *he was dying*. He was sure of it. Body failing, the fire growing, time running out, he'd sent her away.

Could have been with her right then and there.

Fuck, he'd fallen in love.

Later. Deal with it later. He still had to find Lady, once he'd taken out the trash in San Bernardino.

Right here, right now. Standing in Shitfoot's shower, having done exactly what he'd set out to do. Lucky to have run into the daughter, leading him farther up the ladder. The hierarchy of evil. Climbing, climbing, grabbing and throwing off motherfuckers left and right.

He rotated three-sixty in the shower, the water waking him up.

Clumps of blood and dirt melting down the drain. He'd like to peer down in a shower once and not see blood – his own or someone else's. Once. He'd have plenty more blood on his hands before then.

He crouched down for a bottle of gel and held it high, squeezed it on his head, then the rest of him, dropped it, and started scrubbing, foaming up. Groaning, the pleasure of hot water and a foamy soap.

Nothing Lulu might do for him could ever compare.

"You okay?"

Not a peep. Must still be sore at him.

"I promise, no more tying you up, soon as I'm out. As long as you take me to your brother, I'll treat you right. Got some questions for him."

Still silent.

"And about you, like, wanting to help me, or get in here with me, don't get me wrong, you're really cute and all, but I'm kinda seeing someone right now, or was, it's still a fresh wound, see?"

Nada.

"And that mess about your dad, too."

Negative.

Slow Bear washed the soap out of his hair and eyes and blinked until he could see again, then peeked out the curtain. "Lulu Doll?"

She was gone.

"Aw, no no *no! Fuck!*" He lunged for the shower knob and spun it off, slipping and squeaking all over the wet tub. Ripped the shower curtain open, yanked it from a handful of rings. He nearly fell out of the tub, banged his big toe, shouted "*FUCK!*" again, hopped around, reaching for a towel.

Got it.

Wrapped it around his waist, still grimacing from his son-of-a-bitchin' toe. Just what he needed, a limp slowing his roll.

He scuffed his feet across the rug until dry enough to hurry into the hall without slipping. Holding his towel with his only hand and shouting, "Lulu! Lulu Doll!"

The cords were strewn down to the kitchen. The knots were

shit after all. Should've known better, but he'd gotten the big head, thinking he could do it all – kill pedos, save children, not get caught, have nine lives, tie great motherfucking knots.

"Lulu Doll!"

In the kitchen, Slow Bear turned in circles, wondering which way she'd go. Upstairs? Out to the pool?

Idiot. Of course she ran out the front door. Probably already in her car, gone, on the phone to someone who could deal Slow Bear a good whooping.

So close. He'd been so close, he could feel it. Darwin would've led him to Lady, a joyous reunion, and he could carry her to Nebraska with him to check on Abeline and the girls.

"Oh god, oh god, fuck me!"

He squeegeed water from his hair, let it roll down his back and legs. His saturated towel loosened and plopped loudly against the tile.

The front door opened and Lulu's voice chittered away at someone. "Please? Listen to me! He's dangerous, he tried to rape me! He killed my daddy! Knocked my tooth out! Why aren't you listening to me? Let go of me!"

They rounded the corner, Lulu hunched at the waist, because behind her, Toni had wrapped her hand around the back of the girl's neck.

And Slow Bear stark naked. Shrunken.

"Toni?"

Hmph. She shook her head. Six feet of badass poured into jeans and a black leather jacket. "I thought the girl was full of shit, but now I'm not sure."

Slow Bear picked up his towel, held it over his junk. "Good to see you, too."

Chapter 8

Mama drove her cruise ship of a Caddy out of Salt Lake City, down south towards Provo. The sedan swayed and rocked like they were at sea, and Slow Bear had to breathe easy through his mouth to keep from going green around the gills. He couldn't tell if she was driving like an old woman or a teenage girl.

Old woman was unfair, though. A good foot or more shorter than her towering daughter, smooth talker, smooth walker, quick and feisty.

Yeah, call her feisty to her face, see what happens.

Her first question in the car: "So, what are you, anyway?"

"Sorry?"

"Why are you special to Toni? Why does she want to help you?"

"Beats me."

"I won't have any bullcrap, not if you and me are going to get off on the right foot."

"There was a house fire. Not my house. The firemen rescued me, and your daughter tried to take me to the hospital."

"Tried?"

"They wouldn't take me. Too many Covid patients, and they thought I was a creep."

"Mm." Mama cut her eyes at him. "I've seen plenty of creeps, but never heard of none turned away from the hospital over it."

"The house I was at, the guy who owned the place, he made a lot of money hurting little girls, so I killed him, killed the people who worked for him, and burned his fucking house down."

"Language."

"What? Really? Did you hear what I said?"

"For future reference, have respect. You're some sort of

avenging angel, but with only one wing?"

He held up his hand. "Well…I do my best."

She ten-and-two'd the wheel, lifted her chin, and floored the gas to pass a semi that kept swerving onto the rumble strip. Slow Bear braced his feet on an imaginary brake pedal.

"Personally, I'd have told you to let the Lord sort it out, keep your nose out of it."

"They didn't give me the choice."

"Peter sliced off a Roman guard's ear to protect Jesus, but you know what Jesus did? He took the dusty ear and reattached it to the guard's head, then let them take him away."

"Okay."

"But hurting children…who am I to criticize? Besides, sounds like you and Toni was fated to meet."

"How so?"

"When she says it's a Jesus thing, she means it's a Jesus thing. She's never been wrong."

"What's a…what's a Jesus thing?"

She chuckled, nice and warm, the way grannies do. Reminded him Abeline was a grandmother too.

"In all my years on Earth, all seventy-seven of them, I've never seen anyone as sensitive to the Holy Ghost as my Toni. Youngest of four, the only one willing to take care of me after my Morris passed, not even a churchy person, but she knows. Somehow, she knows. If you're a Jesus thing, you are the real deal."

Not what he wanted to hear. Still processing. "I'm no angel, avenging or cherub. I'm no deal. And I sure as flap jacks don't truck with Jesus much. But I appreciate the help."

"You're welcome. But if I die of Covid, I'm going to haunt your sorry butt."

They pulled into Provo, Slow Bear fading, dizzy, seeing double. The mountains loomed, threatening to fall on top of him, snowcaps and all. At one point, he thought they passed a spaceship, but made of gleaming white stone with a spire towering from the middle. Definitely Mormon.

Slow Bear must've dreamed the rest of the way, when the car

floated to a stop as Lady was handing him a beer at the casino bar on the rez. Or was it Nebraska, where Abeline had picked him up at last call, him lucky and her probably not as much as she'd hoped. Lady was long gone by the time he'd met Abeline. In his dream, they eyed each other up over the bar, Lady saying, "We don't serve old bitches here," and Abeline saying, "Your baby-fat ass could learn a trick or two from me about stealing your man."

Slow Bear was never Lady's man. The one big clue it was a dream.

"You still with us, Micah?"

He woke and wheezed. Mama had parked in front of a swanky modern apartment complex, expensive wood trim, steel and glass. Minimalist? Rich people shit, but tasteful, compared to the McMansion he'd torched.

"Here we are. You going to be okay?"

"Are there stairs?"

"Elevator."

He opened the door. "I'll be alright."

But *holy shit* was he ever not alright. Hurt to step out of the car, hurt to walk, hurt to hurt.

They rode up to the top floor, not seeing anyone along the way. The door to each apartment was a huge black slab, a monolith, and Mama took a single key from her pocket and unlocked one of them.

Pushed it open.

Inside, pretty much what you'd expect. Hardwood floors, furniture with an antique look but was probably thrift store finds refinished by whoever lived here. Cheetah, he supposed, whoever Cheetah was.

He noticed no TV in the living room, but a simple but top-of-the-line Bose stereo, a huge CD collection – yes, CDs – and *books*. Books everywhere. Old, new, art, poetry, science, religion stacked on coffee tables, others on end tables, stacks on the floor. The shelves were overflowing with them. Under or around or in the middle of all these books were papers, marked all over in green ink, manuscripts, whatever. Starting to yellow and curl, others pretty fresh from the printer.

Opposite the front door, two glass doors leading to a small terrace, a few loungers, a sun umbrella, and overflowing potted plants.

Mama was winded. She stepped over to the worn leather couch and let it swallow her. "Can you believe I used to run track? Jump hurdles? Now a drive and an elevator wears me out."

The giant door seemed to close on its own behind Slow Bear. He limped over to the couch and eased down next to Mama. Barely enough air in his lungs to talk. "If I make it to forty, I'm not sure how many of my parts will still work. Can't imagine fifty, let alone your age."

"Can't tell if you're being rude or not."

"No, no, I mean –"

Her laugh roiled up. "Just kidding, boy."

He glanced around again. The walls were covered with art, most of it pretty crap, unframed, stained, as if Cheetah didn't care about perfection. Cheetah liked what Cheetah liked and hung it up no matter what. Lots of landscapes of deserts, lots of bad Georgia O'Keefe clones, lots of pictures of nude women, blurred. No, not blurred. What was it? Impressionism?

And, "Hey." He pointed towards a tall canvas between two towering bookcases, the background yellow, but in the foreground, tastefully nude, "Is that Toni?"

Mama grunted. "Cheetah's painting. Another one like it in the bedroom, charcoal sketches framed down the hall. I told her Toni could take them down now if she wanted, but she's not ready."

"You told Toni she could take them down? Not Cheetah?"

Sad smile. "Can't ask Cheetah anymore. Cheetah's gone."

"Like, left gone? Moved?"

The old woman sighed and held up a *one moment* finger. Then she stood and wandered around the cluttered room, moving books, piles of paper, scrolls of artwork, before picking up photos. The old fashioned kind, ones you had to get developed at the drug store. Mama sat beside Slow Bear and picked through shots, handed them over one by one. Close-up of Toni with another woman, a white woman, stripes of white hair through deep ginger, high cheekbones and a smirk instead of a smile. Another shot, wider, Toni and the woman seated at a restaurant table, someone across catching them in mid-laugh. Toni wore a leather jacket over a black turtleneck, while her companion wore a silk blouse, sleeves rolled up. Neither wore much make-up. Neither needed any. Slow Bear guessed they didn't care what anyone else had to say.

"Her name was really Helen, but Cheetah was a pet name, I suppose. Can't remember how long ago we switched from one to the other. Seven years? Six?" Mama's laugh simmered. "Cheetah was a smart woman. Very smart. In many ways. A professor at the university here, you know it? Brigham Young? And she was a Mormon, of course, but not really practicing."

"You and Toni aren't Mormons, then."

"Not a chance. African Methodist Episcopal for life, baby. Not like I've been to church in fifteen years or more. But the Saints, they call themselves Latter-Day Saints, they're nice people. Wrongheaded, but very nice people. Jesus probably tolerates them fine, even if they get on his last nerve."

"But Cheetah was Mormon."

"It tore her to bits, knowing better than to believe all the hoo-ha, her own family spewing her out. Finding Toni, the best thing ever happened to her."

Another photo. Cheetah in a simple cream-colored dress, Toni beside her in a Sergeant's uniform, U.S. Army. Hands clasped, a desert sunset behind them.

"Wedding?"

"I've known for a long time, known since Toni was a girl. You could tell. Took after her daddy. I know it's not natural, I know it, but it's not the same as boys, is it? It's a whole different game. Like I was going to tell her men were better? Not the way I grew up. Not the way her father treated me." Mama shuddered like taking bad medicine.

"What happened to Cheetah?"

"Well...sometimes the girl was too smart for her own good. A Pee-H-Dee, but she'd fall to pieces at the drop of a dime.

When she was okay, she was wonderful, way out of our league on book-learning, but Toni's got instincts. All her life, if she made a choice I wasn't particularly fond of, she'd tell me, "It's a Jesus thing."

"Jesus."

"She meant, you know, Jesus was calling her to help someone. Like you. Same with a lot of people in her life. Definitely with Cheetah."

Another photo. Cheetah alone, must be Toni behind the camera, and sad. Smiling, but still. In a short skirt and thick sweater, arms crossed, orange rock layers behind her. Maybe Zion. More gray hair than in the other shots.

"It was not easy. Not at all. Especially when it was time to move me out here. Toni wanted the three of us to live together, but Cheetah was afraid her family would find out about Toni, and all she'd hidden from them in her life. I stayed with Toni about six months before we agreed to find me my own place, give her more freedom. But Toni was growing frustrated. Told Cheetah she was going to have to start treating their marriage like a marriage, not an illicit affair."

"Mm."

"Right. Both suffering, both made each other happier than anyone else on Earth. It was the one time Toni's instinct failed her, Lord bless. She drove down one night for dinner, Cheetah had said she'd roast a chicken with potatoes and carrots. Then Cheetah didn't answer her phone when Toni started over. Once here, she found a raw chicken on the counter, half-peeled vegetables, and Cheetah in the bath with both wrists slashed."

"Goddamn."

"His name in vain, watch it, now. The note said she'd finally gotten the courage to tell her mom. The bitch demanded Cheetah never contact her family members again and hung up. Wouldn't answer when she called again. It was too much."

Slow Bear wanted to pepper Mama with questions – Was this Toni's apartment now? Was their marriage legal here? Did Cheetah's family not even come to the funeral? Or did they want to fight Toni over her belongings, her burial, and so on and so forth but he a coughing jag was coming fast and –

He couldn't stop. Hardly able to draw breath, nearly knocked him out. Boom. Delivering a Mike Tyson to his head. Again and again and again.

The rumbles quieted and Mama was standing over him, thumping her fists on his chest, lightly, trying to loosen the phlegm.

"Son, if I get the Covid because of you, Lord have mercy."

"You'll…kill…me?"

"Probably won't live long enough to."

"If you do…sorry. I didn't mean it."

She patted him on the chest. "Let's get you healed up. Start in the bathroom, get yourself clean. You are a right mess."

Which was how he ended up in Cheetah's bathtub, same place she ended her own life, wondering if it would be where his ended, too.

Chapter 9

Shitfoot's clothes were too big for Slow Bear. Had to wear his blood-and-brain-speckled jeans and flannel shirt Mama had picked up for him brand new in Provo. The only clothes he had to his name anymore after she'd decided his soot-and-sweat-soaked combo was beyond hope. He kept his old boots, though. Hadn't failed him yet.

He took a pair of the bastard's socks.

The three of them sat outside, the pool lights muddled through the muck, Shitfoot still twirling, and the chlorine still hiding the smell.

Toni's only comment on seeing Shitfoot in the pool: "I've seen worse."

Lulu Doll had crossed her arms and sulked since Toni dragged her inside and heard Slow Bear's story. Whining, "You can't believe him over me! You can't! He had his way with me!"

"Girl, can I call you girl? Anyway, girl, I can tell you, hand on a Bible, even if it catches me on fire, he wouldn't lay a finger on you. Total gentleman."

She leaned nearly doubled-over towards Toni. "He was going to *murder* me, like he did my dad."

Toni glanced between them.

Slow Bear shrugged. "Yeah, she's got me there. That was the plan, at first."

Back to Lulu Doll. "I'm sure he had a good reason."

"Oh, fuck you. Fuck the both of you."

Slow Bear cracked his neck. "For the last time, no."

She sank into her chair, sulking.

While he was drying off and dressing a bit ago, Toni told him because she knew he was going to ask anyway, "After what you told me, you thought I'd let you go alone?"

"Told you the truth, at least. I was too tired to lie."

"Except your destination. I hung around the bus station after dropping you off, waited for you to climb on a bus and start out. Followed you the rest of the way."

"How's your mom?"

"Fine, fine. No harm done."

"Sorry."

"Not your fault. She knew what she was doing."

Shit had gone iffy in Utah.

"Good to hear."

Now the sun had set, they could barely make out each other, and a chill breeze set Slow Bear's teeth on edge.

"Why not kill Miss Doll, then?"

Slow Bear let out a deep breath. His need to cough, a constant companion for weeks, not banging as hard as usual. He cleared his throat. "I thought I'd gone as far as I could go with Shitfoot over there."

"Shitfoot?"

"What I've been calling him."

"His *name* is Trey. Trey Fiskadoro."

"I'll stick with Shitfoot."

Toni asked, "Is Fiskadoro a real name? Or made up?"

"It's as real as any other name. Was David Bowie really David Bowie? Or Elton John Elton John?"

"Hecules." Slow Bear stabbed a finger at her. "Elton's real name is Hercules."

"*No*, idiot. It's Reginald. Hecules is fake, too."

"Hey!" Toni played referee, thrust her arms between them. "I only wanted to know if Lulu Doll Fiskadoro is your actual name."

"Tallulah." Gaining confidence now, pretty sure murder was off the table. "My mom liked old Hollywood names. I got stuck with Tallulah, but no one ever called me Tallulah. It was always Lulu. Dad added 'doll' when, like…*things* started happening. He never dropped it."

Toni turned to the pool again. "Things happened?"

"Yep. Things," Slow Bear said before Lulu could get started. "Bad things, her own dad, but I wasn't going to kill her for that. I was going to kill her because she's actively helped get her dad new girls to play with, and get rid of them when he got bored."

"Seriously."

"I *told* you, I didn't have much choice. My brother, my stepbrother, I mean –"

Slow Bear let her keep on for a couple minutes when a wave of nausea crashed in his stomach. He squeezed his eyes shut and breathed through his mouth, rode it out. So stupid. Acid gnawing his gut, burping up pure rotten eggs, having gotten this far on either dumb luck or divine intervention. The universe was telling him, *Hey, you done good, but you're done, man. Like way past your expiration date.*

Last time he was dead, truly dead, in an airplane fuselage turned brothel in a North Dakota airplane hangar, he didn't know he'd died. A hot shot of heroin sent him out of our world. A few minutes later, he gasped awake when the NARCAN hit his system.

No tunnel. No loved ones. No angel band. No chariots. No ancestors. No flames, either.

Just…nothing.

And the whole goddamn truth of it was…

He didn't mind.

The nausea won and Slow Bear leaned to the side in his chair and started retching. Dry heaves. Fell out of his chair. All fours – no, threes, all threes. Thinking, *Here's your hell right here.*

Toni stood. She didn't go to him. She'd seen him in worse shape before. He was falling apart every step of the way but too stubborn to let go of the pieces.

Several minutes later, he rolled onto his side, curled up. It eased the beast.

He sat up, held up his hand. Toni stepped over and helped him to his feet. He wasn't even sure he had feet anymore.

"Okay, it's simple." Trying to catch his breath. "The girl's going to take us to her brother, Shitfoot Junior."

"*Step*brother. Darwin."

"Her stepbrother, and I want his help to find my friend, the one I told you about, the one they took."

"Someone took your friend?" He'd forgotten to tell Lulu Doll. Bad habit of his, assuming everyone already knew the story.

"Kylie. Took her from me, nothing I could do. They beat the fuck out of me."

"Girlfriend?"

"Friend friend. She didn't deserve what happened to her. If she hadn't been helping me…" He swallowed hard. "If your brother is connected, I'm going to find her and take her home."

"And you won't kill us."

"I won't kill you." Careful to make *you* singular. Like, *I won't kill* you. Because he was abso-Jesus-Fucking-Christ-o- lutely going to kill her brother.

Kill him a *lot.*

Toni rubbed his back. "What makes you think he'll deal with you? What makes you think he won't shoot us on sight?"

Chinned at Lulu Doll. "We'll have her, for one. And also, I'm pretty convincing."

Lulu Doll got out of her chair, stepped over. "If you're serious about not killing us, I'll drive. Like I said, *fuck* Daddy. I'm glad he's dead, and Darwin will be, too, okay?"

Slow Bear nodded. "Deal." Turned to Toni. "You coming along?"

She sighed. "Somebody's got to keep an eye on you for once."

Yeah, Slow Bear thought. *Kill him a whole goddamn lot.*

Chapter 10

Slow Bear remembered…

Cheetah's bathtub, soaking until the water went cold and Mama had to come drain it and refill it. Hot, hot, hot.

Floating away.

Spent time jawing with his grandpa on the front porch of his rickety shack on the rez. Jawing about "Goddamn you and your Kevin Costner movies."

Could've sworn Cheetah herself stepped into the bathroom and eased across the floor to sit on the lip of the tub. As usual with his ghosts, the signs of self-violence weren't hidden or washed away by the Lamb. She was gashed up with blood-stained hands. Wearing a flowing pantsuit, the way Slow Bear imagined women professors might, from what he'd seen on TV and the photos Mama showed him.

Dead, you know. Pale sunken skin, purples blotches where the blood had settled, fogged eyes. Calm. Quiet.

Slow was not sure and would never be sure if he said aloud, "Lovely apartment you have."

She grinned but didn't say a word at first. Very slow movements. He realized, she'd died in the water. She moved like she was still under.

When she did speak, it was…cold. "I wish Toni had never met you."

"I get it."

"You are Death itself."

"She saved my life."

Cheetah sighed. Seemed to take hours. "People who save your life don't go away whole."

The water grew chilly again. Cheetah slipped her fingers into the bath, brushed them around in the water. From chilly to *arctic* right quick. Slow Bear tightened up, started coughing again, tremoring, blacking out.

Mama rushed in, "Alright, alright, you'll be okay. I'm coming."

Cheetah was gone.

Next, he was in bed. Cheetah's bed, Cheetah and Toni's bed. Queen-sized, lush sheets, a warm comforter. Mama must've helped him dress and climb in, but it was a complete blank to him. His breath rattled – *death rattles, death rattles* – and he shook like a quaking aspen in a hurricane.

Too pretty a thought. Too pretty for how he felt.

What if the aspen was on fire?

But he somehow found sleep. Stumbled into it. Big tree root in the woods. Maybe an aspen root. Stop it. Stop. Stop *thinking.* Thinking won't heal you. Thinking only makes you feel more guilty.

He stumbled into sleep, stubbed toes and skinned knees.

Slow Bear woke in darkness. The open door allowed a little light to spill in. Blackout curtains, except for the thin burn at the edges, an eclipse.

And sitting on the bed facing him, arm propping her up over Slow Bear's legs, was Toni.

He said, "I'm sorry about Cheetah."

"Thanks, but you don't have to. You didn't know her."

"I bet she was great."

Toni sighed, turned to the ceiling. "She was a coward. She knew me too well. She knew I'd never get over it, over her. Well played."

"Sorry."

"Say sorry again, I'll slap the living Jesus out of you."

Made him laugh. Grumble.

Toni met his eyes. "So, I lost my job. I guess kidnapping a patient doesn't show good teamwork. Rather than let them scold me more, I walked out."

"Fuck." *Sorry it's all my fault sorry sorry sorry.*

"You were thinking it."

"Prove it."

"It's all good, though. I've got plenty of friends in the healthcare business. I'll land on my feet when I'm ready. But right now, Let's get you feeling up to code."

"Code blue."

"Purple, even. No, violet. I've dealt with plenty of crazies before."

Slow Bear managed to brace himself on his elbows and push up. "What about me? What did they say about me?"

"I told them you escaped. But to that cop, you remember? To him, I hinted I might have left you to die in a landfill."

"No way he believed you."

"Whatever. He didn't contradict me, anyway. As far as I know, no one's looking for you. Everyone thinks you're dead, am I right?"

"Say what, now?"

"Micah Cross? AKA 'Slow Bear'? I Googled you."

"Of course you did."

"A one-armed indigenous guy named Micah, it wasn't tough to track."

Indigenous. The word hit his ears weird, like Nirvana through steel wool headphones.

His elbows wobbled and he collapsed into the pillow. "What did *they* have to say about me?"

"Former reservation cop, fell into depression after losing your arm to a shotgun blast, not in the line of duty. Rumor was you were banned from the rez due to some unspoken crime, possibly murder. They say you set your trailer on fire while you were in it, and you burned to a crisp."

A grin. "They left out a few details."

"Do you plan on telling me what they are?"

The thought of telling the whole story sapped his strength. "I'll think on it. Meantime, what's for dinner?"

Toni shook her head and stood from the bed, started out. "Bullshit," she said over her shoulder. "A big pile of steaming bullshit."

Couple of nights in Cheetah's bed did wonders. Mama helping sometimes, Toni the rest. Chinese, pizza, tacos, and then Mama got sick of the takeout and went to the store, bought steaks, potatoes, and too many veggies, made a big soup out of it all. Pretty good, gave him strength. Covid was still ripping his asshole wider, but slower now. Not coughing as much, not wheezing as much. Able to stand for more than fifteen seconds without feeling the need to collapse.

The kindness of these two, for fuck sake. He'd lucked into kindness along the way, never expecting Abeline to be the wonder she was, or Toni to see Jesus in him. Never expected an old lady cooking him soup.

The third night, sitting down to leftover soup and fresh sourdough, Slow Bear told them the rest of his story. Rez cop, lost his arm to bad fucking oil workers up in Williston, limped along on disability, settlement money, and his "odd jobs," what others called meddling in people's business. How he killed a man who'd shot a couple, a misbegotten love triangle. Instead of pinning a rose on him for it, the Chief whooped Slow Bear's ass and sent him away. Then losing Lady, finding out who was behind it, dying once, dying twice, finally getting his pound of flesh before the traffickers could kill him a third time.

But he wasn't done. Still needed to find Lady. He had to follow the trail of trucks packed with women, against their will and under the influence, to their final destinations. Ask around at all the bars on ladies' nights, or talk to the pervs in the park who were supposed to stay a lot farther away from kids than they did. He chanced upon a real POS named Gerardo transporting two young girls through the Midwest, bound for California, sold like turkeys.

Mama and Toni gave him stone cold stares.

Burnt the dinner rolls.

He cleared his throat. "We ended up in Salt Lake City, where one of the middlemen lived until I killed him and all his friends and burned his house down. Where Toni found me."

Mama and Toni turned to each other. Jaws moving, nothing

coming out. Like, *You talk because I don't know what to say.*

Toni sniffed the air. "Shit!" She grabbed a pot holder and opened the oven. Smoke billowed out, choked her. She grabbed the sheet pan, slammed the oven door, and dropped the pan on the stove. Black-topped dinner rolls.

"I'll take one anyway. Tear the burnt part off."

"Where are the girls?" Mama said. "The girls you said you found?"

"Safe. With a friend. A woman. They're safe."

Toni knocked a knuckle on top of a roll. Hard as stone. She picked up the pan, took it to the trash and dumped it.

"Hey, come on. I wanted one of those."

Mama, wrinkled brows and all, ripped the paper towel in her hands to strips without knowing it. "Lord, Lord, the blood on your hands. Can't you call the police? Give them ah, ah, anonymous tips?"

He shook his head. "Don't trust the police. Used to be one."

Mama turned to Toni, at a loss.

"It's a Jesus thing, Mama. I swear."

The old lady wadded up the paper strips, nice and tight in her fist. "Well, he did beat the shit out of those bankers."

"Traffickers."

"Not you. Jesus. Went into the temple, chased out the bankers. If he can get mean, then I suppose you might be a Jesus thing after all."

Slow Bear thought about the rolls in the garbage, way past the five-second rule now.

Toni crossed her arms. "So, what's next? Where do you go from here?"

"You asking if I'm done?"

"If you want, I can put in a good word with my friends, help find you a job at least."

"Mighty kind, really, mighty kind. But I've got unfinished business out in California."

"Hm," Mama hummed. "Mm mm hm. Unfinished."

"There's a man still expecting his delivery of two young girls. If they don't show up, I suspect he'll order replacements.

So…unfinished business."

Nobody wanted to talk much anymore, at least until dinner was over and they settled down to watch Chicago firefighters, doctors, and cops say and do the most predictable things. Mama ate it up like fro-yo on a spoon.

Another few days of lying low, breathing a little easier hour by hour, the pain subsiding slowly, Slow Bear caught up on the world via cable TV. Out of the loop for a long time, never much watched the news before. Never seemed worth it to hear about wars or scandals he couldn't do anything about anyway.

Watching it now, the numbers scrolling across the bottom of the screen growing exponentially – positive tests, hospitalizations, deaths – while the President spewed ridiculous crap about shooting up bleach. Slow Bear reminded himself not to vote.

He learned about "long Covid," though. Hoped to hell it wasn't his fate. Weakest he'd ever been, even more than lying on the ground outside a meth trailer, his shoulder gone spaghetti, bleeding out.

He learned about the "lockdown," the whole country losing its shit. Can't blame them. Slow Bear wouldn't wish Covid on anyone.

He learned about #metoo, Black Lives Matter, *American Dirt*, Joe Biden's basement, and wokeness.

Those scrolling death numbers, tick tick ticking up up up.

He clicked away to old Magnum P.I. reruns and vegged on those instead.

"Get up, right now. Come on."

Slow Bear woke up to Toni shaking him. He'd made it to bed somehow, couldn't recall how, like a drunk. Hadn't been drunk in a long time. Covid made him remember why not.

"We've got to go, man. Get yourself up. Get dressed."

"Fuck, what's the fucking…the hell is going on?"

"Cops. Cops are coming. Lucky I got a head's up. They'll be here in a few minutes. We've got to get you out of here."

Groggy, world spinning around him, Slow Bear sat up. Toni flipped on the lights and blinded him. Cold shiver ran from his scalp to his toes. "How'd they know? Like, *how*?"

"I'm thinking the asshole who handcuffed you to the gurney didn't believe my story about dumping you. Someone's been watching me. Watching us. Figured it out. Why aren't you dressed yet?"

He grabbed his jeans, pulled them on over new boxer-briefs. Yesterday's socks. Boots. A new t-shirt, his old flannel over it. The desert would kill you a few different ways. Burn you up all day, freeze your ass all night. At least his thick North Dakota blood gave him a bit of defense against the chill.

One in the morning.

He ran his hand through tangled hair, rubbed his tongue across his teeth – like moss was growing on it.

"Okay, I'm ready. What's the plan?"

"You and me, a long drive, maybe sleep in the car. Wait until they forget about you."

"Too late!" Mama shouted from the living room. "They're already here."

Red and blues strobed off the walls of the living room, amplified by the glass doors to the terrace.

Toni grabbed Slow Bear's upper arm. "Hurry."

"Wait, you want to race them down? You know they'll cover all the exits."

"They don't even know who you are! You're dead to them. They don't know who they're hunting."

Mama stood in the bedroom doorway. "You two go on out of here. Get in the closet."

"The closet?"

Toni nodded. "Got it. Don't do anything stupid, Mama."

Rolled her eyes. "Bullies. All bullies can do is bark and snap. You go on and I'll be fine."

Slow Bear wanted to stay, defend her, lay waste to these piggies before they knew what hit them, but a one-armed Indian versus Provo's finest? In his dreams.

He could put *any* town in that spot.

Redneck City's finest? They'd murder his ass.

Portland, Oregon's finest? They'd murder his ass *and* compost him.

"Mama, please, come with us." Called her Mama. Couldn't remember the last time he called someone Mama and it felt like "Mama."

She waved them off. "Go! Go! I'll be fine."

They bee-lined to the door, peeked into the hall. Toni held something in her hand. *Jesus, not a gun. Not pepper spray.* Slow Bear blinked, looked closer. It was a key. A single key.

"Hurry," she said, jogging across the hall to another monolithic black door. She twisted the key in the lock. Opened up, went right in.

The elevator dinged.

"Get in!" Toni hissed.

He dove inside, tripped and landed face down on a hardwood floor, missing a Persian rug by several feet. Dazed. He glanced over his shoulder, the world blurry, but it was another apartment, shaped almost exactly like Cheetah's, except much less cluttered with art and thrift-store finds. It was some expensive blur.

Toni eased the door closed, careful to not make any noise. Clicked into place. Gingerly turned the deadbolt lock, but it wouldn't go. Again.

In the hallway, the elevator door opened and murmuring men stepped out, talking to each other, one talking on his radio, getting curt robotic replies. Toni flattened against the door, swearing at Slow Bear with her eyes.

He shook himself from his fog and crawled to the door, lifted up on his knees.

Toni tried talking without moving her lips. "Duh. Lock."

He pointed to the deadbolt. She nodded.

He couldn't get it to go either.

A couple of fists pounded on Cheetah's door. "Police." Another round of pounding. "Police, I said."

He stood, crowded in on Toni and put his eye to the peephole. His eyelashes got in the way. Barely able to make out a couple of older guys in sport coats and khakis. The other three were uniformed, younger, more grim.

Toni tried lifting the door by the handle, trying to line up the deadbolt.

Clink.

Still didn't work but the noise got the closest uniform's attention. He turned his fish-eyed nose towards the peephole.

Slow Bear and Toni held their breaths.

He couldn't do it for too long. Still couldn't suck enough air into his lungs. His body tremored. He squeezed his eyes shut. The cough was coming. Unavoidable.

Mama opened the door to the police. "What do we have here? What's all the fuss about? Hey, don't touch me."

"Ma'am, we have a warrant."

"A warrant to what? Let go of me, son."

"A warrant to search the apartment. You're harboring a fugitive. You or your daughter. Stand out here with me while they –"

"The hell are you talking about? Harboring? We harboring? Are you out of your mind?"

Mama was *loud.* Toni and Slow Bear spoke without speaking.

I gotta cough!

You cough, we're dead.

I can't help it!

"You don't be touching her art! You'd better have respect!"

"Ma'am, please, don't interfere."

"Interfere? I got rights! I know my rights!"

Slow Bear launched himself from the door, down the hall, dizzy-headed, hoping he wouldn't collide with anything breakable. Who owned this pad anyway? How did Toni have a key?

Wheezing, trying to hold on, he found a bathroom, dropped to his knees, and wrapped his one arm across his mouth and *hacked like a motherfucker.* Muffled his bitch of a cough.

His entire body took the impact badly. Made him want to shout "Ow!" and holler "Mama!" and not care who heard, as long as someone might come along to stop the hurt.

The spasm wound down until he could catch his breath and

open his eyes. He didn't want to move, afraid it would start all over again. But eventually…

He flipped onto his ass and sat up, his world spinning, but definitely Toni standing in the bathroom doorway.

"I got the lock."

Croaked out, "Sorry."

"Smart, running down here. Real smart."

He shook his head. It was instinct, not smarts. "Mama still doing okay?"

"Still yelling, getting other tenants to come out in the hall, white tenants. They're telling the police Mama's good people. It's a mess."

"You said this place was, what, the closet?"

"Stupid joke. If Cheetah's friend or coworkers or, god forbid, *family* ever showed up unexpected, I'd come over here to hide for a while. The couple are retired, spend their summers here. Very nice, very generous. Probably wouldn't want to be seen with me in public, but still, they didn't mind me hiding when they were here, and they gave Cheetah the key to keep an eye while they were gone. They're the ones who told me, 'Come hide in our closet any time.'"

Slow Bear managed to push himself onto the toilet. A smaller cough rattled him, and he muffed it into his shirt sleeve again.

When it trailed off, they stood quietly. Too quietly, listening hard to Mama's shouts of "Bullshit!" and "Harassment!" Other voices joining in, decent neighbors, loud shitty cops, Mama keeping them in check.

Slow Bear and Toni drifted slowly towards the door again, taking careful steps. Ears to the door, face to face.

"Y'all see the way cops treating us? Y'all knew Cheetah. Y'all know Toni. We have every right to be here."

"Not what we heard."

"You heard wrong. You always hear wrong, you cops, you sons of bitches."

One of the neighbors, a man, said, "Detective, there's no reason to treat her like this. We can –"

"Hey, Dustin?" Calling to a uniformed cop. "Yeah, get Dustin over here. Dustin? Can you get some cuffs on Mr. Peace-and-Love?"

"Whoa, wait a second."

"Your choice, sir. Go inside your apartment, or the cuffs."

"It's overreach. I know the law."

"A lawyer? We got a lawyer here? Then go inside and wait for the lady to call you after and retain your services. Don't say another word. Not one more."

But Mama laughed. "Bet you stole lunch money in school. Bet you cheated in every fight you ever won. Pure bullies, all of you."

"Dustin? Cuff her instead."

Listening through the cold black door, Toni and Slow Bear's ears burned. Watched the whites of each other's eyes go red. Faces flushed.

And nothing they could do. Not a goddamned thing.

Slow Bear thinking, *All she'd have to do is turn me in. Turn me in and they'll leave Mama alone. No point in them suffering for me.*

He lifted his hand, ready to unbolt the lock, but Toni snatched it from the air, held on with a death grip. Shook her head. Mouthed, *No.*

Mama's shouts outside, "Y'all see, right? Y'all see? These boys are pussies, they can't deal with a loud-ass black woman without putting her in chains!"

Slow Bear grit his teeth. "I'll kill them."

Toni's grip tightened. Stronger than him. "Save it. She's going to be okay."

"Let me go. Turn me in."

"She's doing it for you."

"I didn't ask her to!"

A little too loud.

One of the uniforms knocked on the door. "Hello? Police."

The detective said, "What are you doing?"

"Swear I heard someone inside." He knocked again, louder and longer. "Police!"

Another voice, a woman from a neighboring apartment. "Oh, no, that's Oli and Jan's winter place. They left last week for Chicago."

"You sure no one's staying right now?"

"No, just them. They'd thought about AirBnB, but changed their minds."

"You've got a key?"

Fuck fuck fuck fuck. Slow Bear tore his hand from Toni's and went for the lock again.

The neighbor lady said, "Sorry, no."

"Swore I heard a voice."

"Fine, go find out from the manager. Dustin, take her inside and sit her down before the whole goddamn building comes up here."

They listened as Mama was taken inside Cheetah's place, the door closing behind them. The suspicious uniformed pig asked the neighbor how to find the manager, and pretty soon the hall was cleared and quiet.

Toni and Slow Bear collapsed, squeezing in deep breaths.

When Slow Bear found his voice again, he said, "You've got to help me get out of town. I'll take a bus. I promise, it'll be the last you hear of me."

"You're not ready. You need more time to heal. And maybe, I don't know, maybe you can think of a purpose other than, like, trying to kill these people. You can't keep killing people."

"They're not people. They're fucking monsters. Monsters. I've seen it, first hand. One of those girls I found? Pregnant at fourteen. You know what they'd do to her if they found out? Don't tell me about not killing them. There's enough dead kids already. I can never make up for it. Never make up for them taking my friend."

"Micah –"

"I appreciate all you've done for me. I don't deserve it. You're the Jesus thing here, not me. And I'm not going to let you and Mama ruin your lives for me."

More deep breaths.

Still more.

The hall still quiet.

Toni sat up. "Well, if we're going, let's go now. We can take the back stairs, hope no one's waiting at the bottom."

She helped him up. They sneaked into the hall, wound around the hallways to a fire exit door, but Toni said the alarm had been disarmed because smokers hung out in the stairwell.

Down the stairs, slowly, coughing along the way.

Outside, across to a big boxy SUV, Honda Pilot, deep blue. Toni's ride. Cranked up, and drove right past the police cruisers and unmarkeds, almost invisible, and on to the bus station.

Chapter 11

Slow Bear slept the sleep of the fucked.

A body needing rest, needing healing, and a soul dropping down the levels of Hell while he dreamt. Reminding him, *You ain't moving the needle. But the needle, your final needle, they're gonna give it to you. It's gonna burn. Fire in your veins til it hits your heart. Why? Because playing God is frowned upon in these United States.*

Unless you're, like, really ass-raping rich.

Like Darwin. Got rich off pedos because his own dad is – *was* – a pedo and somehow turned human trafficking into multimillions with legitimate businesses.

The fuck of it all.

He awoke feeling feverish, but freezing. Gray light in the room with a yellowish haze fading in. Morning. He'd slept at least, what, three, four hours?

Having Toni show up was miraculous. Otherwise, he would've had to stay up all night keeping Lulu Doll from bolting. Or figure out another way to tie her up, knots she would still probably escape unless he used chains and locks and duct tape over her giant mouth. Shove a couple tube socks in first.

But no. Toni was able to take over, and since Lulu didn't think Toni was going to murder her, he could rest easy-ish.

Could, but didn't.

Awoke in the master bedroom, an adult man's room instead of kindergarten nap time. California king, impressive dark wood sleigh bedframe. Dark wood. Sleigh. Probably antique and stupidly expensive. The mattress, probably even more stupidly expensive and high-tech, hadn't done him any miracles. Restless, sweaty, horror-dripping sleep.

Sat on the side of the bed in soaked-through boxer briefs,

wishing he could have clean clothes like normal people instead of torn, filthy, bloodied, stinking, moist…

He rummaged the walk-in closet, found silk boxers too big but with enough elastic to kinda-sorta hold onto his hips. A Versace robe like Apollo Creed or an Arab sheik might wear – lots of gold thread and more silk, bright blue and white and gold. He put it on, the empty arm and shoulder sliding off until he took the belt from its loops and tied it higher, one-handed and with his teeth.

He wandered downstairs, where Toni stood in the kitchen staring out at the pool, mug of dark coffee in her hand. She turned as he came in, the robe swishing against the floor.

"Want me to make you some?"

"I'd rather have…" Remembered there was no orange juice. "Okay, yeah."

She stepped over to the French press on the counter, nearly empty. "I've drained three of these already."

Slow Bear searched around. "Where's the girl?"

"She's fine. I encouraged her to take her dad's Valium, probably what he gave the girls. I put her in one of the rooms with the toys, the kid's bed. Your boy taking a swim," Gestured at the pool. "He'd already safeguarded it for me. Windows sealed shut. Iron bars and screws. The door locks from the outside."

Toni held up a key on a rabbit's foot.

She started the kettle on the gas stove. Slow Bear mounted a bar stool at the island.

"We've been lucky. I don't know if it's always as quiet around here or what. If I hadn't burned all my strength killing Shitfoot, I wouldn't still be here, wouldn't have found out about Lulu, or about Darwin. But someone else might show up eventually. Friends? Services, like a pool boy? Maid? Can't stay too long."

"Sounds like you didn't think this through."

"I didn't get this far on thinking *anything* through. Pure dumb luck and people like you."

"People like what?" Sharp eyes over her shoulder.

"People like you and Mama. I don't deserve it. Should not have survived. Should not be here instead of cuffed to a hospital bed in, what, San Quinten? Heal me up in order to put me on Death Row."

The kettle whistled and Toni poured it over the coffee she'd scooped from the grinder. Fancy. "Why keep going? Let me call the police. Anonymously. There's plenty enough evidence in the guy's house to show them what's really going on. Slip them Darwin's name. Then tell me more about your friend and I'll pass it along. You go take it easy for a while. We can head home to Utah until you're ready to stand on your own two feet."

Grinned. "What about the girl?"

Toni passed a steaming mug across the island. "How about an overdose? Valium and, oh, a couple bottles of her brother's wine. Chardonnay? We can type a suicide note on her phone."

"Look at you, planning murder now, too."

"Jesus cursed a fig tree that wasn't making figs. This girl's as bad as a fig tree."

Slow Bear sipped his coffee – needed a lot of sugar and a lot of cream. He searched the walls of the kitchen until he found the wine rack. "Hand me one of those bottles?"

Toni followed his gaze, turned and grabbed one from a built in rack, bottles held on their sides. Red. Toni glanced at the label then handed it over.

The label was rustic, roughhewn beige paper with torn edges. *Fiskadoro Vineyards* in block letters. An "Evo Red Blend," 2017 vintage. The "Evo" in exquisite calligraphy, the "Red Blend" more of a scrawl, like real handwriting. A drawing, or more like a woodcut, of a famous drawing of evolutionary man, starting with a little monkey, each step another stage, with the last being a modern man holding up a wine glass. Smaller block letters beneath: *Paso Robles. Survival of the Fittest Vines.*

Slow Bear didn't know much about wine. When he used to drink, it would do if there wasn't a better option. Got him drunk faster than beer, not as fast as the hard stuff, and made him sad if he had too much of it. Why couldn't Darwin be into oranges, right? Then at least he'd get a glass or two of fresh squeezed before ending this idiot.

"Pretty, ain't it?" He turned the label towards Toni.

"Motherfucker."

Down the hall, a few thumps on the bedroom door where Toni had stashed Lulu Doll.

Toni crossed her arms. "So, what do we do?"

As tempting as it was to let Lulu Doll die with the consequences of her choices, Slow Bear shook his head. "We need her to get to her brother."

Seeing Toni's smirk, he dropped his eyes to his cup. Barely touched it.

"So, you're still going through with…this…plan, I guess it is?"

"It's almost over. If I can talk him into handing off *one girl*, you know?"

More pounding down the hall, Lulu shouting, "Are you people here? Hell-*OOOO*! Goddamn it all!"

Toni went, "*Mm mm mm.*" Started around the island, heading for the hall.

"Wait."

She paused.

"You don't have to come with. I mean, thank you for it all, I mean it, I swear, thank you. But you should head home to Mama, don't let me drag you down with me."

Couple of seconds? Forever? No difference.

Toni knocked her knuckles on the island, went "*Mm mm mm*" again, and walked off down the hall. Shouted, "Coming, girl. Keep your panties on."

Chapter 12

They let Lulu Doll drive her little Volkswagen hatchback, small but fancy. Easiest way to do it, Slow Bear thought, to give her the tiniest bit of control, the illusion of it anyway. Toni sat up front, even though the car was too small for her. But if the girl went rogue, Slow Bear wanted two strong hands to slap her down, not his measly one.

Lulu Doll kept saying, "It'd be better if I call ahead, tell him we're coming. I don't even know if he's in the country right now."

"We'll roll the dice."

"If he's not home, or at the winery, then what?"

"We wait for him."

"Could be *days*. Weeks." Her cheek bulged after every sentence, her tongue addicted to touching the hole where her incisor should've been. "You don't *show up* in California. Nobody shows up uninvited."

"I'm nobody, so I'll just show up."

"That's not what I…" Trailed off into a pout.

Slow Bear relaxed into the back seat, said, "I know," and turned to watch the scenery pass by. Wasn't much of it. Lots of other cars at first, slow-going, billboard ads, faded highway signs, green like old chalkboards, pockmarked with bullet holes. The space between cars showed paper and plastic trash strewn along the roadside, *strings* of it caught on dead weeds and car-wreck debris, dirty from exhaust when the semi-trucks blew past.

His first time in California. He might not survive it.

He lost himself in the boredom for a while, kind of like meditating. Better than thinking about what was to come.

Finding the words to convince Darwin to…what? Lead him to another trafficker, who'll lead him on and on until someone gets tired of the game and shoots him dead? They all know by now. This isn't the Wild West. This is the future. Cell phones and texts already blanketing the Coast – *This one-armed Indian is hunting us. Kill on sight.*

Kinda sorta listening to Lulu Doll up front trying to drum up sympathy.

"I'm glad he's dead. I wish I'd had the nerve to kill him myself when he was molesting me." She hit the word *Mo-LES-ting* hard. "It's like a cult, you know? They scrambled my brains. I didn't even realize what I was doing until *he* showed up yesterday. He rescued me."

Toni went, "Mm hm."

"He saved me, he really did. I owe him."

And so on.

Until the traffic filtered away, the sights and sounds outside softened, the sky an abstract painting over the hills. The roads narrowed.

Not long after, the vineyards. Row after row after row after row…

He'd never seen a landscape quite like it.

Slow Bear had been born and raised smack dab in the middle of North Dakota. Rocks to the left, rocks to the right. Prairie grass, brown and tan mixed with scant green. Brutal winters. Brutal summers, too. Worst of both. There's a beauty to it, of course. Except he took it for granted. Everyone takes their home turf for granted. Boring, dull, doesn't matter where it might be. He would've bet these Californians rolled their eyes when someone mentioned the Pacific Coast, or Hollywood stars, or *this*, all *this*, laid out before him. Grapevines, green hills, cool air, perfect warmth, and a Van Gogh sky, for fuck's sake. Made him hate Californians a little bit more than he already did.

He stopped taking the rez scenery for granted after his arm was shot off and he was useless as a cop, his side-hustles pointless without a badge. He climbed on top of his vintage (i.e. seen better days) Richardson bi-level mobile home, which he'd dragged out into what he thought was ownerless land far away from the city lights, nearly every night to stargaze, his eyes getting better at it, seeing more, deeper, wider, darker.

He missed his trailer. Blew it up in order to get away scot-free. It convinced the tribal police and "The Hat" he'd killed himself in the fire, giving him freedom to chase Kylie and her kidnappers across our great nation without having to face the consequences of all the stupid shit he'd done to get into this mess.

Still, the view…wow.

On the last road before the winery, the car twisted and turned up hills, a narrow red dirt track between two vineyards, flashing by. Slow Bear guessed it was the rear entrance, for employees – "servants" – so the wealthy patrons driving up the grand, wide, paved road to the main parking lot would not have to mingle with the help. Be a shame if the gardener's work pick-up dinged a CEO's Porche.

The roof of the main building appeared over the crest, a different vibe than Slow Bear expected. He was thinking antique, fancy, European. But with a better angle, more like someone had said *Modernist Horse Ranch* and thrown all their money at it.

A lot of weathered wood, exposed beams, and glass. First, they'd need to clear the seven-foot black slat fence surrounding the place. Lulu Doll pulled up to a gate, stopped. She held out her hand, palm up. "My phone, please?"

"What about it?"

"I need my phone to open the gate."

Toni gave the girl a few blinks. "You're lying."

"It's all app these days. Better hurry or they'll figure out something's wrong. They're watching us right now."

"So, tell Toni the number, she'll type it in for you."

Eyes up and to the right. *So bored.* "No? Okay? That's not how it works anymore?"

Upspeak hit Slow Bear's ear like a cheese grater.

"First, you go to the randomizer. It pops up a one-time code. I type the one-time code into the app. Gate opens. Easy peasy."

A thought hammered Slow Bear: *Bad idea bad idea bad idea.*

But the whole farce was a bad idea. And now Toni was

involved. He'd never forgive himself if she got hurt out here.

"Give her the phone."

As promised, Lulu Doll *type-type-typed* and the gate opened, and she parked in a small lot, a couple of Suburbans and Vans marked with *Fiskadoro Vineyards* on the sides, an alien spacecraft with a "T" on the trunk, plugged into a weird-looking gas pump. No, not gas. He'd seen these. An electric outlet. The future, eh? Electric cars, but they'd burn through a shit-ton of oil making the plastic for those weird pumps with the plugs.

And as he expected, a line of beaters. Old, dented, rusty. Pick-up trucks, cheap imports, bad rims and scratched paint. The people who made this place run smoothly.

They climbed out of the tiny car and stretched, Toni kneading her lower back muscles. Slow Bear thought Lulu Doll acted less nervous already. He could tell she'd been here a lot more than she'd let on. Spider and fly, letting Slow Bear get tangled up so much he couldn't break free of the web now.

A few men in sports coats over golf polos appeared out of thin air, it seemed, walking towards them. All three in thin blue surgical masks. One older with a paunch, only enough hair to see the remains of his defeated hairline. The other two, chiseled bro bods, younger. Checking out Lulu Doll from behind shades. The older one was more interested in Toni and Slow Bear, giving them a *you don't belong here* gaze.

Slow Bear grinned and faux-saluted.

"Lulu, you've brought guests?"

She pointed at Slow Bear. "Micah." Then Toni. "Toni. Visiting from out of town."

"Okay, and?"

"Thought I'd share a couple bottles with them."

"Did you, now?"

She crossed her arms. *Don't fuck with me.* "What are you trying to say, Gideon?"

"Not on the list today, is all I'm saying. You didn't call ahead."

"Since when do I call ahead? I'm family."

"But with guests? You think you can waltz in here with

anyone?" Turned to Slow Bear. "Who are you supposed to be?"

"Crazy Arm."

"What?"

"You know, like Crazy Horse? Except…never mind. Most people call me dead. Otherwise, Micah Cross."

Arms akimbo, Gideon planted his tongue behind his teeth, sucked. Then swiveled his head toward a bro. "Ask what Mr.Fiskadoro wants to do about them."

"*Do* about us?" Lulu Doll tore off her sunglasses. "*Do* about us? Gideon? What you *do* is let me in to my own family's place, like you *do* your job and shut up. How long have you worked here? Because I think I belong here a lot more than you."

"I've never been kicked out, though."

"One time."

"No, many more, but you don't remember the others. You had…different friends then."

Slow Bear peeked at Toni, a flutter of a grin. She'd probably have no trouble taking Gideon's head clean off.

The bro who'd murmured into his cell phone hung up and tapped Gideon on the shoulder. A clipped, "They're good."

"Well, then." Gideon rubbed his palms together, one two three. *I wash my hands of thee.* One of the bros handed him three surgical masks, which he passed along. "Put these on and follow me, please."

Sure, masks. You show Covid who's boss. Like taking a chess piece to a knife fight, but if he had to wear it to meet Darwin, fuck it. Let's roll.

Chapter 13

Slow Bear had to hand it to Darwin Fiskadoro. The winery was pretty cool, a real vision behind it – not overly gaudy, not the bad taste of "bigger is obviously better" Hollywood rich types, but also not too modern, not overly minimalist. Open door policy. Welcoming almost everyone (except blacks, Hispanics, Asians, Indians of all shapes and sizes…unless they were employees), a sort of high-class Cracker Barrel.

Their path led them around a small pool next to a couple hot tubs – for the staff, Lulu said – and then through the kitchen. Mexican line cooks put the finishing touches on what looked like raw cat food. A grill shot flames as grease dripped down, but all Slow Bear could identify was giant mushroom caps, charred like steaks. The smoke smelled nice – mesquite – and reminded Slow Bear he needed food. Wished he could fatten up in one big go and hibernate like the animal he was named for.

Hallways lined with framed photos, good times on the grounds, with lots of wine glasses held aloft, clusters of white people smiling, having fun. Framed awards. Gold something, Silver something, Sparkly-foiled numbers in the nineties.

Then the bros pushed open saloon-style doors into a wide lobby with a glass wall taking in the hills, the vines, the glory of it all. Racks full of wine bottles, ceiling to floor, counters with several couples or groups of friends enjoying "tastings" as particularly adorable women behind the counters put on a show for the guests. The sort of women who'd try for the "best friend" or the "ex-wife" roles, but regardless of their gorgeous smiles (which Slow Bear couldn't see due to the masks), sensual curves, and quick wits, Hollywood still frowned upon them as, "Too

Midwestern."

Maybe Slow Bear was just horny. A short brunette with a pixie cut and oversized glasses across the way poured pink wine while talking about "Ro*zay*," looked up for a moment and blinked at him. He guessed she wore a plastic smile beneath the blue mask.

Been a long while since he and Abilene shared a shower in a Colorado hotel right before it all went to hell in a stolen van.

No, the girl wasn't smiling at him.

The bros held open two large glass doors and Slow Bear shaded his eyes with his hands, the tint of the glass deceiving. Out here, on a huge wooden deck full of sun-brellas and long picnic-style tables, everyone encouraged to sit together, make new friends, share their shockingly expensive bottles with strangers, and maybe the whole she-bang turns into a Roman orgy. Why not?

But now? Covid times? Black cloths covered every other table to enforce the six foot rule.

Gideon had them sit at the end of one of the long tables. The bros lingered close but not too close. All around, pods of people, masks on their wrists or weighed down on the table under wine bottles, enjoying the sun and cool breeze, taking in the majorly non-inclusive view, pouring deep purples and crisp pinks and bubbly sparkling into glasses, all shapes and sizes.

"So, Lulu." Gideon turned on charm so phony it smelled like chemicals. "What can I bring you and your illustrious guests this fine afternoon?"

She glanced across the table. "Any favorites? No worries about price. I like the Sauvignon Blanc, the 2014. Yes, do you have any 2014 left? Yum. Gideon, yes, one of those, and?"

Raised one of her eyebrows like Spock. *Fascinating.*

Toni shrugged. "I don't drink much wine."

"A Cabernet, then, definitely, the king of reds. Oh god, if you like red. Do you like red, Micah?"

Slow Bear lolled his head towards Gideon. Caught the nasty glare in his eye. Reminded him of a dude from Williston he'd enjoyed killing. Manfred. Another flunky thug. "Got any orange juice? Extra pulp."

Oh, his fucking sneer. "I'm afraid we don't. We *do* have a young orange wine, though. From 2017, a wonderful bottle. We call it 'DNA with a Twist.'"

"Is it like orange juice?"

Lulu giggled.

"No, you see, it's not *made* from oranges, but the coloration is on the orange, red, pinkish –"

"Pass."

"We have some local craft lagers and ale, and we make our own session IPAs, both hazy with an IBU of –"

Fucking headache. "Water. A bottle of water, Sealed. Better poke a hole through the screwtop."

"Me too," Toni said.

Gideon bowed while twirling his hand to the side, stretching his arm. What a douche. He walked off, speaking into the Bluetooth device in his ear. So small Slow Bear hadn't noticed until now. Pretended like he had authority, had the bros "call in" for him, but he'd been taking orders direct from the top all along.

The bro-hunks stood their ground. What did they get paid for this gig? Did they really know what they were doing, or hoping a visiting film director would say "*You'll be a perfect ineffective bodyguard for the next episode of* NCSI Blue"?

"Isn't it great?" Lulu Doll flourished towards the view – which Slow Bear guessed would be dotted with other wineries, hotels, and spas before too much longer. It's grapes bringing people here. *Of course* developers try to build shit on the land other than more grapes, meaning, eventually, fewer grapes, and thus, the grapes move to another part of the state and the whole clusterfuck starts over again.

"What do we do now?"

If Lulu Doll was paying attention to him behind those sunglasses, he couldn't tell.

"Lulu?"

"Can we please…can't we all sit here quietly for a minute?" She rubbed her fingers under the shades, wiping away tears.

For her dad? For herself? For Darwin?

Surely not for the girls whose lives she'd helped destroy.

"We're sitting ducks," Toni whispered.

"I know."

"And she's the cheese."

"Ducks like cheese?"

"No, I mean, we're mice and she's the cheese."

"We have the *best* cheese here if you'd like some." Lulu turned to them again. "We partner with an organic creamery. Even their vegan cheese is good. Oh, here we go."

Gideon headed over with two wine bottles by the necks and two glasses by the stems, upside down, in his hands. But a few steps ahead of him, a younger guy, hard to tell his age because of his wealth. A decade older, Lulu Doll had said. His face had a timeless sort-of Brad Pittiness to it. Dark hair, though. Shaggier than it should be, like he was going for Tom Cruise in M:I2. Black dress shirt, opened one-button too many. Jeans, faded and dirty kind of like Slow Bear's own, except Darwin probably paid for his to come pre-crappy.

Cowboy boots. Again, subtly filthy.

He had a bottle, too.

Gideon had dropped the fake bravado, another hired hand under his boss' gaze, Darwin's expression was honest-to-god *natural.* Not a smile, not a grin, but not a sneer or frown either. Absolutely no reason for him to put on a mask – figuratively and literally.

This dude did *not* rattle.

"Sis, an unexpected surprise. How are you?" He set the bottle on the table and took the space beside her on the bench, gave her California air kisses on both cheeks. Chaste. Slow Bear thought if these two were fucking, or had ever fucked in the past, neither gave the game away. "And friends! Great! I had a feeling something like this would happen today."

He reached his hand out to Toni, who took it without thinking. "Darwin Fiskadoro, pleasure to meet you. Hope you're enjoying my winery."

Then did the same to Slow Bear.

But his left hand.

See, the normal way to do is right hand to right hand.

Obviously Slow Bear was down an arm, and easy to tell which one.

Meaning, Darwin was fucking with him.

Which meant…

Slow Bear didn't bother lifting his hand at all. "Micah Cross. Yesterday, I killed your dad and left him floating in his pool."

Toni's eyes went wide. Lulu Doll yanked off her sunglasses, pouty-lipped, probably because she'd planned on dropping that bomb in another minute or two.

Even Gideon paused for a long moment from opening the bottles and pouring the wines.

Darwin nodded. Elbows on the table, hands clasped. "I know, yeah, I know. And thank you for it, by the way. Saved me a lot of money from having to pay Gideon to do it."

Gideon's fingers slipped and he cut his thumb with the corkscrew, sucked the blood away.

"You *knew*?" Lulu Doll, with her inimitable dramatic flair. "You mean…you could've…he was going to *murder* me. Not even rape. Straight up *murder*. And you couldn't have warned…I mean, I was doing the errand for *you*…"

She shut up when she put one and three together.

Hid behind her sunglasses again.

Darwin kept on, "I'm surprised at you, Micah. From what I'd heard coming out of Utah and North Dakota, you are a true terror. Or were. Did she try the 'my stepbrother blackmailed me into having sex with him' angle? I figured she would, but guessed you wouldn't give a shit and off her anyway. Gee, Lu, you talked your way out of it. Impressive."

Lulu shrunk before their eyes. "Jesus, Darwin. Love you, too, bro."

"Well, 'love' is a bit much. Not like we're blood. Guys, I never touched her. Our dad didn't either. My stepmom told me she was concerned, she'd known what he was into all along. I went in action. It was porn with dad, then 'favors' for clients, quid pro quo their teenage daughters. We saw what was coming. I did what I could to protect my little sis by giving him substitutes."

He grinned at her. "And this is how you repay me? Telling him your hog crap story about us?"

Through her clenched teeth. "He was going to *mur-der* me."

He held up surrender palms. "Okay, fair enough."

Slow Bear was plenty used to being behind the curve, in the dark, grasping at straws. It had become his whole danged lifestyle. Still, Darwin knowing about Slow Bear's coming and goings…unexpected?

A vast and hollow understatement.

Whoever Slow Bear had pictured out here on top of the exploited girls' pyramid, it wasn't Darwin.

Lump in his throat.

"The girls?"

Darwin took a slurp of wine, a real assholey sort of slurp. Then, "The girls. The one move you actually pulled off. Pretty smooth, Ex-Lax, pretty smooth. But no victory lap for you, sir, since we've got our people out in Nebraska zeroing in. Any day…" Checked his giant gold-and-diamond watch. "Any *hour* now."

Slow Bear was on his feet before he realized. Hand an inch away from Darwin's throat when Gideon grabbed his wrist and wrenched his arm behind him, another guard piling on from behind, forcing his torso to the table. Wine bottles, glasses scattering, breaking, slicing, *stabbing* into Slow Bear's chest, stomach, *fuck fuck fuck*!

Darwin had barely moved, but his shirt was drenched purple. He'd held his glass up and out of the way. Took another slurp.

Everyone else at the table had leapt to their feet, jumped out of the way.

"Mercy, Micah, you could've hurt yourself. Or maybe you did. Glass stem to the heart?"

"You're not that lucky."

Darwin flicked his chin at Gideon. The two goons climbed off Slow Bear and released his arm. Not broken. God only knew what shape he'd be in if they'd broken his arm. He rolled off the table, tried to steady himself, ended up on his ass.

Most of the glass shards didn't make it through his shirt, but a few big and sharp enough punctured the shirt, his skin, poking out. Slow Bear plucked them. Blood ran, yes it did, but nothing dangerous. The wounds would turn jammy and stick to his flannel, as good as a bandage.

Darwin went on like his shirt wasn't fucked. "Even Batman couldn't win every time. Bane snapped his back. Everyone told me you were indestructible. Shitting themselves, scared silly. I was like, *relax*. He not Bane. He's Batman. Batman doesn't have superpowers. He has to piss, eat, and sleep like everyone else. He has good days, bad days. The only reason he's still alive is because he's *fictional*. Batman tries his comic book shit in real life, dead within a week. Think about it. You've got a better track record than a real Batman."

A woman pushed through the front door, carrying a towel over one arm, another white shirt on hanger, two fingered hooked through. Brunette, slender, about forty, tight jeans and hiking boots. Darwin got up, met her in a few steps, pulling off his shirt as he did. She traded the towel for his shirt, waited for him to spot himself clean, then retrieved the towel. She handed him the clean and pressed shirt. He slipped into it, and the woman left with the towel, ruined shirt, and hanger.

How'd she know? Slow Bear hadn't seen Darwin signal. Gideon neither. Nor the bros.

Guessing Darwin had the whole joint wired for sight and sound, 4K, THX quality. Plans B and C in place. Slow Bear imagined a closet full of white shirts, weathered jeans, and cowboy boots, pre-scuffed.

And sniper rifles aimed at all their heads.

"Problem is," Darwin said, buttoning up. "You are not fictional. You aren't rich. You haven't shot up any super soldier serum. If I were you, I'd chill, man."

Slow Bear stared him down.

"Chill," Another sip. "Or leave, Micah. Chill or leave."

Slow Bear didn't feel like getting up from the pavement. "Just like that?"

Shrug. "I mean, Gideon here would be happy to escort you. I'll tell him where to take you, and it'll be a scenic drive, followed by a quick pop to the back of the head. You won't even notice. A twenty-two. Almost as sweet as a heroin overdose. Know what I mean?"

Slow Bear nodded. Neither Toni nor Lulu Doll had sat again, watching and waiting. Lulu with her arms crossed, twirling a loose piece of hair. Was she chewing gum? When'd she get gum?

Slow Bear said, "Who is Bane?"

"Excuse me?"

"I know Batman. Who's Bane?"

"You don't know Bane? Big hulking guy, pumped up with chemicals? Broke the Bat's back? Tom Hardy played him in the movie."

"No clue." Turned to Toni. "You?" To Lulu. "You?" To Darwin. "If you'd said Joker, sure. Or Penguin or Riddler, or Catwoman, I know Catwoman, but she didn't kill Batman."

"The Joker wouldn't *kill* Batman. The Joker *needs* Batman. They all need Batman."

"What, they get off on Batman catching them, over and over and over? Like anyone besides the Riddler leaves riddles…"

"Whatever. Don't worry about it. Bane broke Batman's back, put him out of action for awhile. But that's comic books. That's movies. That's not you."

"Sounds like a shit analogy."

Darwin giggled a little. Not a full-on laugh. A guffaw? A hardy-har-har? Slow Bear grinned, not at the giggle, but at the thought of Darwin joining his dad facedown in the pool, faceless and swirling in the chlorinated whirlpool.

Lulu Doll broke the tension. "Micah, tell him about the girl."

"There's a girl?" Darwin's eyes widened. Fucker was enjoying himself a bit too much.

"He came out here searching for a girl. If you help him find the girl, he said he'd let you alone. Micah? You promised."

Might as well, even though Slow Bear didn't plan on letting him alone, and Darwin didn't plan on letting Slow Bear alone either.

"Friend of mine, kidnapped up in Williston. They kicked my ass good and whisked her away, kicking and screaming."

"Taken, you say?"

"Kidnapped. Trafficked. Taken. Whatever the fuck. I'll keep my promise. You find her for me, let me take her away with me, and maybe I'll let you live. For now."

Darwin couldn't keep still on his bench, turning to and fro. "This is about a girl? Your whole vendetta? One single girl? Maybe you *are* Batman."

"Tell him, Micah." Lulu Doll knelt beside him. As if she still thought Slow Bear was on her side. She'd fucked up enough already, concocting those stories. He couldn't blame her, except he could and did. "Tell him about Lady."

"And she's named Lady?" Darwin went all arch-villain on them. "My my, Lady. Indeed. It's a fairy tale."

"But," Toni said. "You know how fairy tales end, right?"

"Happily ever after."

"And a witch in the oven."

Darwin's grin flatlined. He nodded, snapped his fingers at Gideon. "Get Mr. Cross a room, clean him up, get him a new shirt, some shorts. Tell me who he's after, and I'll see what I can find out."

"Sir?" Gideon, dry-mouthed. "Really, sir?"

"Take our other guests to the pool bar. On the house, whatever they want."

Darwin started through the doors, leaving Gideon grinding his teeth.

"You heard the man." Lulu Doll clapped her hands twice. "Chop chop."

Chapter 14

More soft, rolling hills in haze, vineyards full of grapes. Cabinets and pee-nots, meer-lots and Charlemagne, maybe Thunderbird and Dawson's Creek, too. Slow Bear would much rather have a pitcher of fresh-squeezed Valencia, Sweet Naval, or Tangelo.

Good as his word, good as Lulu's promise, Slow Bear was on his way to meet Lady. Sitting shotgun next to Gideon, with a roid-raging bro in the backseat. Pockmarked face, thin chinstrap beard, Bono "The Fly" sunglasses. His every exhale a stunted growl.

They'd retreated to one of the suites on hand for private events – bachelor parties, bridal parties, corporate retreats, bored rich people with a week to kill – and let Slow Bear clean himself up, put on a Fiskadoro polo shirt and a pair of khaki cargo shorts, awkwardly paired with his boots and black socks. Treated him like a guy who'd pulled up in a beater, but had a wad of damp cash in his pocket. Even though he didn't, and he didn't.

Darwin showed up at the suite, sat him down at the table, and said, "Well, we're in luck."

We're.

We're in luck.

Douchebag.

"She not one of ours," *Bullshit.* "But I can get you in. I'll even pay for the twenty minutes myself."

"Twenty minutes?"

"She's not one of ours, I said. Nothing I can do about sending her home with you. But at least you can talk to her, find out she's doing alright, and go home satisfied."

What the living fuck?

"No deal."

Another one of the Darwin shrugs, an affect. Very Elon-ish. "Listen, they're doing this as a favor to me. It's my ass if you fuck it up. What I'll do, I'll give you an escort, Gideon and another guy, H-Bomb. You're going to love him. H-Bomb. He's a real dude, man."

He knocked his knuckles on the table, one two, then stood, extended the wrong hand to shake again. Slow Bear didn't break eye contact, didn't reach.

Darwin rubbed his palm on his jeans. "Alright, you go see your girl, have a good time, and we'll talk later."

Off he went.

Leaving Slow Bear with an angry gut.

But before Darwin stepped out the door...

"Where's my friend?"

He turned. "The one you came with? The tall one?"

"Her name's Toni."

"She's my guest. We'll feed her, give her another bottle or two of our best wine, let her lounge by the pool if she wants. Don't worry about her."

"If you hurt her –"

"Pfft." Darwin wanked the air. "If I hurt her, you can't do squat about it, jackass. But I'm a man of my word, for the most part. She'll be fine, waiting for your return."

Slow Bear bit his tongue. Literally. Tasted blood.

Darwin wasn't done. "You really would've killed Lulu? If she hadn't told you about me, you'd've killed her?"

"I said I would, didn't I?"

An absent nod. Lingering. "Not the worst idea, another spill to wipe up. Hey, no worries. Like I said, go with your girl and we'll talk later."

Now here he was, watching the gorgeous Paso Robles landscape drift by while Gideon spoke quietly on his Bluetooth headset to someone, somewhere. Sounded personal. H-Bomb back there – Gideon called him Serge once, a slip – inhaled and exgrunted like a metronome. Played his role to a T.

Slow Bear thought about what Darwin had said.

Don't trust him.

Don't trust.

Don't.

Of course not. Dude said "Man of my word, kinda."

How many girls has he told they'd be fine? How many had gotten pregnant, forced to abort the baby and keep right on going? How many had gotten sick, Hep, Chlamydia or AIDS? Or dope sick?

Man of his word.

His word was "shit."

And yet, here was Slow Bear on his way to see Lady. He wouldn't believe it until she was right in front of him. Until he could touch her, look into her eyes, hear her say his name.

Otherwise, fuck, they could push him out of the car and run over his head. Another dead Indian, probably a "migrant worker," dead on the roadside. Who'd care? Who'd even pause to finish reading the scroll at the bottom of the TV screen, waiting for NBA scores?

They slowed down on the outskirts of a town, a green sign announcing *Fussin Isle*, but it was no isle. A shocking departure from the peace of the vineyards, everything going concrete and train tracks and potholes, going run down and boarded up, or fly-by-night check-cashing, garbage car buyer rip offs, vape shops – THC oil!

He wouldn't call it blight. More like "slight," working class, clean but crumbling, trying hard, unable to hold back the tide. The mom and pops had evaporated, the motherships of CrapMart and ShitCo landing dead center, taking up what used to be good farmland, and what might be again when the place re-re-gentrified into more vineyard playgrounds for the rich and listless, driving out the guy barely making his mortgage no matter how much THC oil he sold from the little strip mall shop he'd been proud of opening barely a handful of years ago.

Or, you know, it was a laundering front for a cartel, as bad as the big money-sucking bad boys from corporate.

Cynical much?

They pulled into the parking lot of a sprawling ground-floor-only motel, the kind construction workers stay on long jobs. Several cement trucks, a couple semis off to the side, flatbeds full of front loaders and excavators. Only a handful of other cars, pick-ups, one mini van. Gideon guided his RAV-4 into a spot beside a topless Jeep Wrangler, the driver topless as well. A black guy in camo pants, sunbathing with his shirt off. Tight muscled chest, abs, shoulders. In sunglasses, his hair short but natural, untidy. In the passenger seat, white dude in a Corona t-shirt one size too small for his beer belly. Bucket hat with Miami Vice colors and shapes. Red-cheeked.

Gideon lowered his window. "Here he is, visitor for Roulette."

Roulette?

The driver nodded, but the passenger guffawed. Fucking *guffawed.* "Riding the roller coaster, is he?"

"Pardon?"

The driver, couldn't tell which way his eyes pointed with those shades on. "Roulette, never know what you're going to get with her. Depends on the day, depends on the drug."

"Sounds sexy." Gideon turned to Slow Bear. "What are you waiting for?"

Slow Bear climbed out of the vehicle. The Jeep passenger climbed out of his. Gideon and H-Bomb – Slow Bear thinking of him as D-Boob – followed. Only the jeep driver stayed put.

"The money?"

"I Venmo'd it," Gideon said.

The driver lifted a big honkin' iPhone from the cup holder and thumbed it a few times. "It's there."

The chubby white guy, his uniform - cargo shorts and flip flops, led them towards the motel. "Right this way, sir. Hope you're ready for chills and thrills."

When Gideon and H-Bomb started after them, the driver came to life. Up and onto the pavement in a snap. "Whoa, whoa. You didn't pay for no foursome."

Gideon curdled. "Fuck no, do I look like –"

"One at a time, anyway."

"Listen."

The driver reached into the Jeep, picked up a cheap nine from the floorboard. "One at a time, no discounts."

"I said *listen*, bruh. Following me? Listen. I'm not going *in* with him. I'm not trying to make myself sick today, thank you very much. But someone's got to stand outside and wait for him."

"You don't concern yourself. My man Fat Loon here will handle it."

Fat Loon. Guy's name was Fat Loon. Wasn't even really fat. More of a partially inflated party balloon. Fat Loon. Balloon. Fine.

H-Bomb got up in the driver's face. "Our package here means a lot to Mr. Fiskadoro. VIP, you dig? I'm not letting him out of sight."

"Tell Mr. Fiskadoro I don't give a shit. He can take it up with Mr. Wall."

Another name. Another trafficker? Slow Bear didn't know the name. Fuck, too many to keep track of. Mister Wall, farther up the ladder than Darwin? On the list for later.

Who was he kidding? There *was* no later. The rest of Slow Bear's life could be measured not in hours nor days, but minutes.

He didn't want to waste any of those minutes talking to these posturing clowns. His stomach was in a double-knot already. His jaw clenched.

The driver stepped off from H-Bomb – probably due to the body-spray fog – and grabbed his giant phone again. Thumbed it. Held it to his ear, then turned away and mumbled into it.

Gideon flipped his sport coat over his holster, rested his hand on the butt of his pistol. Slow Bear wished they'd waste each other, speed this along.

Instead, the driver signed off and turned around, unphased by the appearance of Gideon's gun, and said, "Stay outside with Loon. Comprende? Leave your gun."

"Like hell I will."

Driver held up his phone. "Mr. Wall on speed dial, I'm telling you. We play by the rules. Fiskadoro does, too, and you know it. Loon's strapped, though. He's got you."

Fuming. *Fuming*. Gideon sighed and slip his pistol from his holster. Dropped the clip and jacked the one from the chamber.

Handed over the piece.

The driver took it in two fingers like he might break it. "We'll be gentle."

"Fuck off you piece of –"

"Hey!"

They all turned to Slow Bear's outburst.

"Can we fucking go already?"

H-Bomb and Gideon trailing them, Fat Loon led Slow Bear down the row of steel doors and giant windows, most of the curtains closed. A few doors were open, a glance revealing girls sitting around in bikini tops and cut-off denim shorts, yoga pants, chattering in Spanish, Thai, Russian, broken English, and native English, the lazy teenage tic *like, like, like* standing out in every conversation. Blasts of arctic air from each room as they passed.

The closed doors, though: padlocked.

Fat Loon flip-flopped on while talking over his shoulder. "The Roulette Roller Coaster. I mean Russian Roulette. Jesus, I swear, give her any drug she'll take it. You want her mellow, shoot her fentanyl or H. You want her bucking like a bronco, smoke up some crack, meth. Goddamn, she's a monster. Couple times I've rode her, shiiiiit. Thick ass, man, been pried open by cocks three times big as you'd think. The whole time, she's talking dirty, *daring* you to get her off. Taunting. Whoa, boy, it takes all types, you know?"

Slow Bear wanted to curbstomp the motherfucker, make him choke on his own blood. But he needed Lady more. Telling himself, this prick, trying to talk her up. Seal the deal. He wanted a satisfied customer. He hadn't been warned in advance who Slow Bear was, really, and why he was here. Another "special guest" of a fellow trafficker seeking a new hole to fuck.

If Roulette really was Lady, then she was only doing what she could to survive. As soon as she saw Slow Bear, he thought, it'd be like old times and they could *go home.*

"But, listen, a few months ago, someone got her high on flakka. Jesus, flakka, real zombie shit. Only a few of the girls here ever tried the stuff, and most of them don't last long. But Roulette, fuck, she's even stronger now, wilder. Like trying to fuck a greased pig wanting to bite your balls off. I don't know, man, she thrives on this shit. If I were you…" Fat Loon dug in his shorts pocket, came out clutching a few small joints. "I'll sell you these, help smooth out the experience, you know?"

Slow Bear gave those joints a look, raised his eyes to Fat Loon, made the dude go weak. Fat Loon backed off. "It's cool, man. No problem. Straight-edger, I get it."

Gideon curdled his face. Slow Bear starting to think he liked boys. Nice clean upstanding rich boys. "How can you even…? The smell alone. And how many trains run straight through them, but you still take a piece?"

Loon grinned. "Don't know what you're missing. Practice makes perfect. We've got newer models, gently used." He pointed to a couple girls across the way, neither older than twelve, had to be. "They start slow."

The henchman shook his head. "No thanks."

H-Bomb's gaze lingered on the girls. Gideon slapped his arm. "No thanks goes for you, too."

Another few doors along, Fat Loon stopped, *knock-knock-a-knock-knocked* at room forty – a "4" and a spot where a zero used to be. "Up and atom, baby. Time for romance."

The door was padlocked, too, but had been beaten to shit. From the inside stabbing outward. Like a wild boar bashing it over and over.

Fat Loon fit the key into the knob and twisted and removed the padlock. Skittered away like he was afraid of whatever beast was inside.

Could be a trap. Could be it wasn't Lady at all, but a nasty *Goodfellas*-style plastic-tarped up room with butchers inside waiting to carve Slow Bear to strips and dry him for jerky.

Fat Loon pointed towards the door. "She's all yours, champ."

Gave the d-bag another eye-to-eye as he approached the door, gripped the handle.

Opened.

Stepped inside.

Fat Loon shouted, '*You're welcome*!" as he clicked the door shut behind him.

Then the sound of the padlock clicking into place.

This is what you wanted.

Chapter 15

The room was glaringly bright from bare-bulb lamps, the shades gone. A king bed, sheets in a jumble, streaked red all over. Trash on the floor, mostly junk food wrappers and bags, crumbs everywhere, ants marching all over. Used tampons overflowing from a plastic ice bucket. The smell of…fuck, what was it? Sex and puke? Rotten food and tequila?

The table was covered with powder, a couple glass pipes, dirty needles, cheap lighters, crushed cigarette packs.

Enough.

He heard her chittering first. Not a laugh, not a sob. Like a squirrel. Chittering.

In the bathroom doorway.

Filthy, head to bare feet. Yellowed toenails. Down to skin and bones, but still wide-hipped and big-titted. Her hair, short like a boy, but matted.

The freakiest thing, though, she wouldn't stop moving. Straight-armed, jagged steps in place. Teetering. Jerky. *Zombie.*

"No more no more no no no leave it to me leave it to me, leave leave leave…"

"Lady?"

"You want me? You want to fuck? Fuck me? Want to fuck? Want a *wiiiild* ride? Want to?" She staggered, turned, leaned over. Her ass large, thin boyshorts, deeply stained. Her shirt was too tight and too short, as if seared to her skin.

She finally lifted her head.

Her eyes, wide, wild, evil.

"Want to fuck me? Want to fuck me? I'll fuck you. I'll fuck you. You got candy for me?"

Slow Bear grit his teeth. His temples, throbbing. His throat tight, strangled.

"Kylie?"

She stood straight, then bowed deep, like throwing herself to the floor, stopping short. And again. And again. "I'm Roulette. I'm, yeah, I'm, yeah yeah, I'm Roulette, spin the wheel. Bet on red. Always bet on red red red."

Slow Bear crushed the space between them, grabbed her by one shoulder, wishing to almighty Goddamned God he had both arms. The stench of death wafted off her. Up close, the eyes were worse. Trapped in her own private hell, reigning in it.

"Kylie! It's Micah! Look at me! Stay with me!"

"Micah? Micah? Slow Bear? My Micah? My Micah is dead. But but I'll pretend. I promise I won't tell I won't. We role play, okay? You be Micah. You cut off your arm."

"Focus, girl, focus! I'm Micah, I'm really Micah!"

He didn't have much grip with only one hand, and she wheeled away. Yelping. Gasping. Staggering more, her arms straight and swinging, her hands curled, fingers arched, nails black, bloody, infected.

She staggered to the bed. Crawled on, all fours, knees spread. "Let's go! Be my Micah! Want it, want your cock, want it bad, want it!"

Slow Bear let her pose, let her awkwardly try to pull her shorts down one-handed, her tramp stamp, a teenage lark, scratched to hell, streaked with scars and pus.

They were watching. He knew it. They were watching, a camera set up, or a hole in the wall from the room next door. Watching, laughing, telling each other, "Watch this stupid motherfucker."

Watch him.

By then, Gideon must've told them more, told them Slow Bear wasn't long for this world, one last hurrah in the sack with an old flame before oblivion.

Lady, thrusting her ass backwards. "*Let's go, let's go, let's go…*"

Slow Bear eased one knee onto the mattress beside her, his hand gripping her neck.

Leaning close to her ear. "It's really me. Concentrate.

Remember, the casino. The rez. Orange juice."

"Orange juice." She giggled. "Orange juice."

"Yeah, I stopped drinking, remember. Nursed a beer forever, chased it with fresh squeezed orange juice. Remember, got my ass kicked? You drove me to Williston."

She turned to him. "My car? Where's my car?"

"Nebraska."

"Nebraska?"

"I traded it for a Caddy."

"Where's the Caddy?"

"I traded it for a van. Listen, you and me, we can get out of here." Very quiet, hoping they don't hear. "You and me."

Lady shook her head. "I can't. I need my shit, man. I need it. I need to ride it down. Man, shit, man, my shit, man, my shit, you hear me? You get me?"

Too loud. She'd tip them off.

"Lady, Kylie, stay with me here. It's Micah. Good ol' Micah. I'm so sorry I let them take you. I'm so sorry. I promise, I'll get your shit. I'll give you all the shit you need. These guys, fuck these guys."

"I fucked all these guys. They give me the shit if I fuck them. I fuck them all."

"I'll give you the shit and you won't have to fuck me at all. I'll give you the shit and you can enjoy it."

Her eyes. Draining bile, regaining light. "I wanted you. I liked you, Micah. Why didn't you like me? I would've fucked you, you know? You would've liked me more."

Running out of time.

"I always liked you most. You don't have to fuck me for me to like you. I like you as much as I could like anyone. Believe me."

She clouded over again. Slow Bear saw missing teeth, dark spots in her mouth. Toxic breath. "Do you…do you have my shit?"

Chapter 16

Felt like forever between now and the time Lady was stolen from Slow Bear, the two of them trying to sleep in her beater Ford Fiesta in a WalMart parking lot in Williston, North Dakota. Dragged out of the broken driver's window kicking and screaming by a man with a serpent tattoo running the length of his whole arm, up to his neck.

His buddies pulled Slow Bear from the car and commenced to kick the living, dead, and zombie shit out of him while Lady shouted his name.

She'd been a chubby girl, barely out of community college, making a nice starter wage at the rez casino tending bar. Her tits got her big tips. Slow Bear had sat before her nearly every day after losing his arm, taking permanent disability, but still earning a few poker chips playing barstool Sherlock.

Until he killed a killer.

The killer – well, he'd been a pretty straight arrow guy before – who'd come to Slow Bear asking if his girlfriend was cheating.

Of course she was. With her own husband, because he got off on her cheating. They both did.

The killer did what jealous killers do and killed the husband *and* the wife.

And Slow Bear killed him, tying a nice neat bow on the whole thing.

Except the cops didn't want a nice, neat bow. They wanted fewer dead bodies.

Thing was, the police chief – a cousin of Slow Bear's, believe it or not – and the tribe's current president, "The Hat," thought it a grand opportunity to turn him into a cheap sort of unofficial undercover agent to spy on a former tribe member who'd made a fortune in oil.

To make it believable, the police chief fucked up Slow Bear nice and pulpy on the casino floor.

It was Lady who drove him to Williston, risking her job, and stayed by him as he blundered through his meeting with the exile Santana. Slow Bear, who never said he'd be a good James Bond, didn't just tip his hand. He showed Santana all the cards.

Slow Bear figured *mission successful* and they tried to spend the night in Lady's car, aiming to return to the rez in the morning and sit on his old barstool accepting the odd poker chip now and then.

Instead, Santana decided Lady would make a fine sex slave, stealing her from the car, sending her off to sunny California with a truckload of other girls – stolen Indians, Somalis, Hispanics, white girls with bad habits, and a few Thais specially flown in from overseas.

It took him a while, but Slow Bear eventually killed Santana, his right hand man, the fucker with the zombie hand neck tattoo, twin Eastern European traffickers named Gerardo and Frank, a whole Carl's Jr's booth worth of traffickers including a couple women, a fucking Mormon trafficker middleman, everyone who worked for the prick, and, most recently, Shitfoot.

Along the way, he'd fallen in love with an sixty-year old redhead, saved a couple girls from the trafficking ring, caught and survived Covid, escaped the cops with the help of Toni because it was a "Jesus thing," and finally granted a "last wish" visit to Lady's hotel room, only a step or two above literal Hell.

Even the Devil his-own-fucking-self would turn up his nose at this hovel.

Slow Bear knew the following:

1. Gideon was going to kill his ass as soon as he was done with Lady.
2. Lady couldn't go on living like this, not when it was his fault she was here in the first place.

3. Toni was his "collateral," an innocent by-stander being held hostage at Darwin's winery to make sure he doesn't do anything stupid.
4. Darwin knew a lot more about Slow Bear than he realized, which meant Abeline, Pia, and Melody were not as safe as he believed.

Fuck.

What would Toni tell him to do?

He murmured, "It's a Jesus thing."

Lady tilted her head. "Are you Jesus?"

It really *was* a Jesus thing, wasn't it? Didn't even take Slow Bear believing in the man to make it obvious.

He climbed off the bed. Disgusted. Hand on top of his head. Putting on a show.

"Fuck!"

A knock on the door. "Ten minutes."

"Fuck! Motherfucker!"

Thinking, thinking, thinking.

Thinking was something Slow Bear wasn't good at.

But *doing*. Doing was another story.

He rushed to the bed, climbed over Lady menacingly, grabbed what little was left of her hair and jerked hard, making her gasp.

He whispered, "Do you trust me?"

"Micah?"

"Do you trust me, Kylie?"

Chattering teeth.

A voice from the other side of the door. "Don't get too rough! You break her, you die!"

"Kylie!"

"Yo-oo-oo-u…never called me by my name."

"*Lady*, my special bartender *lady*. Do? You? *Trust*? Me?"

"Yah-ah-ow. Yeah, yeah, okay."

He tried to shield all of it from wherever the camera was, and hoped he was right.

"If you trust me to get you out of here, it's going to hurt."

"Okay."

"Bite me."

"What?"

"When I let go, no matter what I say or do to you next, you're leaving with me today."

She nodded as best she could.

"Bite me. Scratch me. Attack me. Go for the neck. Okay?"

"O-ow-okay."

"Here we go."

Because sometimes, stupid was the only choice we had left.

Chapter 17

"Fucking whore! You're gonna do it, you hear me? I swear, I'll bust your teeth out and lube up with your blood!"

Slow Bear let go of Lady's hair and she went apeshit.

Knocked him right off the bed. Knocked the wind from him. She kept right on scrabbling, no fingernails left to streak him up, she bent over and bit the Holy Mother out of his neck.

His scream was *real.* Hot blood flowing down his skin. Hoped she didn't nick his jugular.

He shoved her off, reached down, picked her up by the throat. Held her in the air.

"You fucking *bit* me! You bit me! You cunt!"

She kicked and screamed and tried to pry his fingers off her neck.

"Help, oh god, help, shit shit shit!" Gargling, dying.

He slammed her down on the table, scattering the dirty needles, the lamp the trash, all of it. The lamp cracked open on the floor.

Hoped to hell they'd hurry up. He couldn't do that to her again.

Slow Bear heard the key slip into the padlock, shouting from the other side of the door. "Sick fuck'll kill her! The fuck, man? Hurry!"

The door flung open, Slow Bear told Lady, "Take em out, any way you can!"

H-Bomb grabbed Slow Bear from behind.

"She bit me! Gonna catch AIDS or shit now!"

Slipping and sliding, H-Bomb's hands not able to keep up.

Gideon's voice, right outside the door: "Alive! He wants him alive! Don't shoot!"

Quick peek at Loon. Sure enough, he had his gun out, huge snubbie revolver. Excellent.

Slow Bear yanked and wobbled, "Swear to *fuck* I'm going to kill the cunt!" and yanked and wobbled and got H-Bomb off-balance, slammed into him with his back, aiming in Fat Loon's direction.

Bowling pins, the both of them.

Slow Bear bounced up, but H-Bomb grabbed him by the arm, nearly pulled it out of socket. He was onto Bear, now. Understood his game.

"Lady!"

She was crouched on the floor. Slow Bear wondered if he'd gone too hard on her, really hurt her. Shit. One shitty last stand.

Then she spun on her heels and leapt to her feet, a shard of broken lamp in one hand, and the other was a fistful of dirty needles. She let out a war cry and hunched over Fat Loon, trying to free his gun hand from under H-Bomb's ass. He swatted at Lady with his free paw, "No, fuck no, *fuck* no! You want you candy, you'd better not even think –"

Too late. Lady pinned his mitt under her knees and took the shard and the needles to his eyes.

Must've hurt.

Dude sure screamed like it must've hurt.

Lady stayed on top of him, grinding and stabbing, grinding and stabbing.

Duuuuude.

Slow Bear's arm was still twisted up with H-Bomb, who tried to slap Lady off Fat Loon.

"*The gun! The gun! Shoot the bitch, please!*"

H-Bomb reached under his own ass, trying to free the revolver from his own bulk, when Slow Bear slammed his forehead into H-Bomb's nose.

Slow Bear's pain reverberated around his skull six, seven times. But he slammed it again. Broke the motherfucker's nose. Collapsed it. A geyser of blood and snot.

Then a muffled but still too close gunshot.

Slow Bear, throbbing. Fucking throbbing. Couldn't focus. H-Bomb's blood dripping into his eyes.

H-Bomb: "My ass! My ass!"

He tried to push himself up, fell over. Writhed around. Slow Bear saw it then, where Fat Loon had squeezed the trigger and the slug ripped H-Bomb's ass and thigh to shreds.

Fat Loon had his gun free, swinging the hunk of metal around, slamming it into Lady's head, once, twice, then realized it was a gun, not a hammer, and –

Slow Bear stepped on H-Bomb's stomach, trampolined off and grabbed Loon's gun wrist as he'd shoved the barrel into Lady's chest.

Pushed it straight down, down, down.

Fat Loon fired.

Straight into his own balls.

Chapter 18

It shouldn't have worked.

Could be more to this "Jesus thing" than Slow Bear thought.

Could be Jesus *loved* himself some manslaughter.

Fat Loon shot himself in the balls, his shorts exploding like a balloon full of wet red paint, while H-Bomb was bleeding badly from his ground chuck leg.

Slow Bear had the gun now. Wished he didn't need it.

Lady blinked at Slow Bear, cheeks puffed and red, mascara streaking down. But they were her eyes again, the demon washed away by a good dose of murderous adrenaline.

She reached for him and fell off Fat Loon's bloody lap. He caught her and held her tight as he could with one arm and a gun in his fist. Buried his face in her neck.

"God, I let you down."

"I should've fought. I shouldn't've let them."

"It's all my fault. All of it. I'm sorry it took me so long to find you."

"You never stopped looking."

"I can't…I can't believe…"

"Me neither, me neither."

"You okay? He hurt you?"

"My head hurts. It's okay. It'll be okay."

It went on another minute.

Before Slow Bear realized.

It shouldn't have worked.

Because why hadn't Gideon intervened yet? He'd been right outside, shouting at them to spare Slow Bear's life, because it wasn't theirs to take.

Where was he?

He broke the embrace and stood, both H-Bomb and Fat Loon's yelling down to sharp moans and hard breaths.

Slow Bear shot H-Bomb in the face. Stepped over to Fat Loon, shot him too. He died with a sharp piece of molded plastic lamp and used needles sticking out of his ruined eyes.

Slow Bear's ears went into a tunnel, a faint ring on the other end. Lady clasped her hands over her ears.

Aimed out the door, expecting to find Gideon drawing down already. Mr. Bear, meet your maker. They can call you "No Bear" in Hell.

But he wasn't there.

Option number two, the dick had run off to his car and gotten the fuck out of Dodge. On the phone to Darwin, spilling the beans.

Outside, a bunch of the other trafficked girls stared in, mouths open, expressions numb. Dead eyes. All darker-hued, all too young.

Slow Bear stepped over Fat Loon's body, his hearing still deep under. Slow steps towards the girls at the door. They parted, opened a corridor.

On the walkway beside the rooms, Gideon lay flat on his back, more girls all-around him, their eyes on the man like he was a freak show exhibit, until they turned their zombie eyes to Slow Bear.

He peered down on Gideon. Long gone.

The girls had overpowered him, even though he had a gun, now on the concrete above his head, thick with blood. They'd overpowered him and stabbed him with every sharp thing they could find in their rooms. Hairbrush handles and toothbrushes sharpened into shivs, pieces of their own lamps, shards from bathroom mirrors, all sticking out of his neck. More pierced his eyes, same as Lady had done to Fat Loon.

Slow Bear's heart sank.

Without Gideon alive, who the fuck was Darwin going to take out his fury on?

His heart thumped harder, deafening down in the depths, but

as he rose to the surface, another sound. A mermaid singing.

Higher still. Slow Bear shook his head. Opened his jaw, swallowed.

The mermaid turned into a familiar voice. A song from long ago.

A girl singing about kissing Valentino by a clear, blue Italian stream.

The fuck?

It stopped. Repeated.

A ringtone.

Gideon's ringtone, coming from his pants pocket.

Slow Bear leaned between two of the girls, "You mind?" and, gun still in his grip, thumb-and-pinkied the iPhone mini from his pocket.

Private number. Of course.

Just another manic…

He crouched, laid the gun on the concrete. Was about to answer the call when Susanna Hoffs cut off. Shit.

Lady stumbled out of her room, hands to her head, moaning. A few of the girls rushed to her, helped steady her before her legs buckled.

In the middle of a…

Private number.

He wanted to go to Lady instead, but at least she was still moving, talking, while the girls fanned her, petted her.

He answered. Tried to imitate Gideon, but he was no good. "Yeah?"

Didn't stop Darwin from barreling on. "You coming back soon? If you want to dump your trash beforehand, fine by me. I can take care of the extra baggage here, no worries."

Speechless.

"Hear me?"

Slow Bear cleared his throat. "Sure, sure. Got it. Will do."

Now Darwin was speechless.

A long moment of silence, all the girls around the henchman's body calmly watching Slow Bear, all those open mouths. Undead.

Unimaginable pain these girls must've been hiding under layers and layers of heavy dope and mental scars.

Darwin said, "Where's Darwin?"

Shit.

"Right here, if you want to talk to him."

"I do."

"Do you believe in ghosts? Maybe try a psychic."

"Really? Think it's funny?"

Slow Bear almost apologized. It was not funny. It was fucking hopeless. Dude flat-out admitted he was going to "take care" of Toni. If Slow Bear tried storming in, guns blazing, with only Lady and a pack of pissed-off feral ex-sex slaves…slaughter. It'd be a fucking slaughter.

"Let me, um…let me talk to Toni."

A bark of a laugh. "Like you're going to order me around now. Do Liam Neeson."

"If you hurt her –"

"What, you'll murder me with your particular set of skills?"

"If you hurt her –"

"It's all your fault, you know. You're the one who brought her here. I didn't seek you out. Everything that's happened or will happen is on you, bro. Not me. All you've done is give us something to laugh about for an afternoon. It's been fun."

Hard swallow. "Let me talk to Toni."

"Fine, sure, hold on. Here she is."

A moment of rustling, passing the phone along.

Then, "Micah?"

It was definitely her. Alive and well.

"I'm here. Listen…I'm real sorry." Barely able to get through it. "I should've never…"

"Did you find your girl?"

He glanced over at Lady. Crying, but free. "Yeah."

"She okay?"

"She will be, I hope."

"You kill anybody?"

"Yeah, had to." Pause. "It was a Jesus thing."

A dark, bubbling laugh. "Now you get it, see?"

"I'm going to come get you, I promise."

"Stop, Micah, don't even. I already know what's next. You know where I'm at right now? I'm sitting poolside, a glorious pool. You would not believe it. I'm sipping a daiquiri. They brought me fish tacos. Ever had fish tacos? Mahi mahi?"

"Can't remember. Don't think so."

"They're really good. I know you tried." A few wispy breaths. "Don't believe what this motherfucker says, it's my own fault I followed you. I'm the one who freed you, hid you, and took care of you, me and Mama. Your soul is clean, boy. You done good."

"Toni, no."

A tremble crept into her voice. "Tell Mama what happened, okay? Tell her I was okay in the end. You can even tell her I repented over liking women, if it'll give her peace."

"Toni."

"I've got to go now, Micah. I've got to…Okay, okay, here, take it back. Wait, wait! Wait!" A scuffle on the other end of the line. Toni shouting, her voice farther away now. "*I forgive you motherfuckers! I forgive you! You still gonna burn, but not me! Not…*"

Next, a blood-curdling scream. Other voices, no doubt Darwin's bro squad. *Shut up, bitch! Down on your knees! Get down, I said!*"

He couldn't stand hearing it. He couldn't make himself stop.

A full-on Taliban-style beheading is what it sounded like.

Hold her still! Hold her! Who's got the knife?

"*I forgive you! I forgive you! I-*"

More scuffling. Toni's voice vanished. Grunts. Heavy breathing.

Darwin lifted the phone again. "I guess we're both going to need a psychic now."

Click.

Slow Bear's hope flickered out like a match. He dropped the phone, fell on his ass, and stared ahead, mouth agape, same as all these girls.

Chapter 19

How long did Slow Bear sit among the girls, imagining Toni's last moments again and again and...

How long?

One of the older girls – twenty going on fifty – shook him by the shoulder. "Mister? They're coming."

"What?"

She shook harder. "Hey!"

His hearing had mostly returned, and he heard the warbling sirens in the air. Police on their way. Lucky he'd always heard them in time to get away. Like a sixth sense or something. Fine luck to get away because the cops never made it in time.

Curious.

Slow Bear closed his eyes. Deep breath. Not the time or place. Needed a dose of reality. *Toni's dying* was *reality.* He flicked his eyes open again, snorted, and clambered to his feet, supported by the older girls.

Lady was standing again, which was good. He waved her over, and she padded across the concrete, wrapped her arms around him and squeezed like a Valencia orange.

One of the older girls, missing most of her teeth, said, "You need to get out of here, get her out of her."

"Right, right." Still not all with it. "What about all of you? Go on, get out of here. You're free."

She grinned, but there was no light in it. "If the police send who I think they will, like, they're our regular customers. They get freebies and cash to turn the other way. They bring us dope they confiscated."

"Jesus." Bile in his mouth. "What about the kids? The little kids? I can take some, pile them into the car. You hide some of them now, and I'll come get more tonight."

The girl reached over and pet Lady on the head. Gently, gently. "We know who you are, we know what you did. They all know you out here. You don't have to save us all, you know."

"I can kill the cops. The ones getting freebies."

"Mister Bear, listen, you don't get it."

"Nothing to get. Go, now, all of you. Take his car." A nod at Gideon. "Get as far away from here as you can."

She moves her hand from Lady's head to Slow Bear's face. "You're a sweet man. A sweet, sweet man. Don't worry. Other cops will come, the detectives. Ambulances will come. Social workers. The bad guys don't get a choice. The little ones will finally get help, I guess. They can go home, or go to foster care, or end up in the system, whatever. The rest of us…"

She looked over her shoulder at the girls, the older teens, their faces and mouths wrecked by meth, their bodies wrecked by men, slackjawed and dead-eyed.

"Nothing's going to happen. Maybe they take us in, try to clean us up. Maybe they try to charge some of us. Maybe. But, what can I say?" Shrug. "We like the dope. We don't like when we ain't got any. Someone else will give it to us. Or Fat Loon's bosses will send new guys, find a new place to work, and…don't worry about us. It's what it is."

Slow Bear couldn't take it all in. Took a step out of the girl's reach. He'd been hooked on H after he'd lost his arm. A hard climb out of Hell, but he did it. "Ever tried orange juice? Saved my life."

Squinched her eyes. "What?"

"Never mind."

"You two have got to go. Get her out of her, man, hurry up."

"I need…I need keys. I need car keys."

The older girl waved over one of the teens exiting Lady's old room. She stepped over, held out her hand, closed. "Catch."

He held his lone hand under hers. She let go. Gideon's car fob.

"Now," the older girl shoved Slow Bear. "Go!"

Slow Bear, with Lady still clinging to him, rounded to corner to the parking lot, remembered the Jeep's driver had stayed out here, waiting for them. He braced himself for gunshots.

Instead, he found the girls had spilled out to the lot as well. Six of them, one shot in the gut. Sixteen, maybe. Two other girls held her head in their laps. The girl flicked her eyes up and down. "Mama? Mama? Is my mama coming?"

The other girls: "She's coming, hold on. It'll be okay. She'll meet you at the hospital."

But when they glanced up at Slow Bear, he knew – she wasn't going to make it to the hospital.

On the ground beside the Jeep was the driver. Bludgeoned. Neck bent far to the side. His gun nowhere to be seen. No doubt already hidden somewhere a girl in need could get it easily if necessary.

"Come on." He led Lady towards Gideon's car.

Stopped. Thought about it. Modern cars, easy to track, computers and shit.

Darwin already knew too much about him, got too close to home talking about Abeline and the girls. Couldn't risk it.

He tossed the key fob to one of the girls tending their fallen friend. "All yours. Where's the jeep key?"

She pointed at the driver's body.

Slow Bear knelt and fished a big ring of keys from his pocket. Good lord. Had to be keys to the rooms, the padlocks, probably more padlocks to storage containers and lockboxes and garages, anyplace he could hide cash, drugs, and guns. Lucky the Jeep key nub was a thick and wide motherfucker.

He headed to the driver's door, climbed in. Expected Lady to already be inside, but she stood in the parking lot, hugging herself.

"Let's go! Cops on the way!"

She shook her head. "I don't know."

"We don't have time. Get in, let's go, come on, come on!"

"I'm worried, Micah. Worried is all."

"Worried about what?"

"What…what if I get sick? What if I need help?"

"You got me. It's me, Kylie, *me*. I'll help you. These people will never bother you again."

Shy eyes. She wouldn't look at him straight on. "Not that kind of help."

Slow Bear's stomach squeezed tight, cramped.

Dope, you idiot. She means dope.

Bullshit shorthand all junkies use. None of them willing to say, "I want more heroin because it's awesome. Give me more heroin."

Always couched in something else.

Same shit he pulled when he was on it.

It *solved* his problems. Didn't cause them.

It *fixed* his pain. Didn't exacerbate it.

Exacerbate.

Not a friend in sight to hold his one-and-only hand when he decided to kick it cold turkey. One cold, fresh-squeezed glass of OJ at a time.

"Get in, Kylie."

"You promise? You ain't lying? You'll get me some?"

"Get in, Kylie. I'm not leaving without you. Get in or a drag you by the hair and throw you in."

She got in.

Not fucking happy about it.

Slow Bear peeled out, passed a few squad cars on the way.

They drove east.

East. The opposite of manifest destiny.

Chapter 20

"I swear." Lady pawed him from the backseat. "Pull over. Be with me. I'll make it worth it. I promise. I'll let you do anything you want to me."

Slow Bear kept the needle on the speed limit. Not worth getting picked up now. Fast enough Lady wouldn't try to jump out, though.

He'd thought she might, several times now. Pull into a fast-food joint for a bathroom break, she wanted to bolt. He'd started sticking to Jimmy John's only. Dope dealers didn't much hang at Jimmy John's.

They'd ditched the Jeep in Nevada after Slow Bear boosted a thirty-year-old Cutlass Supreme out of a dude's yard. He'd only been asking four hundred anyway, according to the soap on the windshield. Four hundred? No one was going to make a fuss over a four hundred dollar Oldsmobile.

At first, Lady'd been relieved, thanking him, telling him she'd never forgotten him. Almost a childlike quality to her. As the hours and roads stretched on, she'd gotten irritable, itchy, "Gotta puke, Micah. Gotta puke now!" Three pukes in two hours, lucky she made it out of the car, into the desert scrub.

Slow Bear told her, "It sucks. It's going to suck. It's going to suck for months. But it *will* get better."

He didn't believe it. She could tell he didn't believe it.

"Help me, please. I promise, when we get home, I'll go to rehab, I swear. Hope to die. But not yet, not now. Shit, man, it *hurts*."

"No. That's final."

"You can fuck my ass. You know you want to. See?" On her hands and knees, working it. "You and me now, I won't let anyone else have me. Come on. You won't even have to do the work. I'll sit on your lap. I can make it *feel good*."

Like a whole other person, letting those words fall out of her mouth. All grown-up, her body for sale, mostly to the lowest bidder. Hot stank breath in his ear, her hand on the other side of his head, playing with his earlobe. "You want me. You've always wanted me. You wanted to kill those guys in the casino, when they stared at my tits or my ass. Like you wanted to kill them. Don't tell me I'm like your little sister. All I need is one, *only one*, you hear? Not asking for a lot. One high to get me through tonight, and I'm all yours. Everything you've ever wanted. I'm yours, baby."

He couldn't help the tears building up. He swallowed them down. He couldn't help the semi in his shorts either. After all, she was right. He'd wanted her about as bad as he used to want heroin, when having one arm was a fucking waking nightmare, twenty-four/seven. When the stitches were still fresh, the flesh still angry, his nerves set off like a hair-trigger. The phantom hand he swore wanted to strangle him at night. He could still feel it, and it closed around his neck, and he couldn't breathe, and he didn't want to sleep no more.

The doctors upped his Oxy, and when it still wasn't enough…shit, finding H on the rez during the oil boom was easier than Jesus cloning all those loaves and fish.

Nobody kicks it forever, though. Slow Bear was patiently waiting the day a beautiful syringe full of black tar would slink its way into his life, once again, and he would be defenseless, once again. The phantom hand itself might be the one doing the honors. A *big* dose to celebrate his homecoming.

But not tonight.

Sun setting, slipping below the horizon, purples and oranges and reds – which would look much cooler high, he had to admit – with midnight black melting down from above.

"Kylie, please, get some sleep. You need it."

Another blast of stank. "I'm great at sucking cock now, I can make you cum in ten seconds, or I can hold you off for a solid hour of pleasure. Get me one hit."

Sex was like another credit card in her junkie wallet. If one got rejected, she moved on to the next.

The next was Anger Express.

"You motherfucker! Worse they are, kidnapping me, but they had dope! What you got? You got nothing! I want out."

"No."

She slapped her hand lazily over the seat. Her jagged nails kept nicking him.

"I hate you. I hate you, I fucking hate you, I *hate you! Hate you! HATE YOU!*" Then she ran out of breath. Sobbed. Another minute or two passed, then, "Pull over, let me go. Please, let me go."

"Nothing but desert."

"Fuck you. Someone'll stop, someone'll pick me up, and they're going to love me right. They're going to treat me like a *lay-dee*. You call me Lady but you won't treat me like one? I fucking hate you so much! *Fucking HATE YOU!*"

She reached her hands around the headrest, overlapped her palms under his chin and jerked up and to the left and to the right all while screeching *Hay-ay-ay-ay-ay-ay-ay* louder and harder than any high note Freddie Mercury had ever hit in his entire doomed life.

Slow Bear couldn't shake her off, weaved wildly across the lanes – lucky they were empty – but finally slammed on the brakes, sending Lady crashing to the floorboard.

It didn't phase her. She sat up and scrambled at the door handle, fell out onto the highway when the door swung wide open. Wobbled to her feet and set off into the dark bramble.

Slow Bear did the only thing he could – eased the Olds to the shoulder, put it in park, and waited.

He wasn't going to buy her anything. No H, no crank, no fentanyl, no X, not even fucking Oxy, and especially not those goddamned bath salts. Flakka. Some scary shit. No, he wasn't going to pimp her out so she could get the high she craved. Wasn't going to turn his head while she did her *thang* at a truck strop or, god forbid, a Taco John's.

A few months prior, Slow Bear had believed she was lost

forever. Vanished. He'd followed breadcrumbs that got littler and littler until he was left following vague scents and gut instincts that grew vaguer and more gutless until he was left following only blood lust.

Then he'd found a new reason to keep going. Thinking of those girls, Pia and Melody, thinking how they would've ended up at a hotel like the one they locked Lady in, once Shitfoot had been done with them. Thinking about Abeline, fierce woman, a one night stand turned into, Jesus, he couldn't tell you right then. Couldn't even explain it to himself.

Hoping they were okay. He'd avoided calling to check in, pretty sure someone was peeking over his shoulder. Turned out he was right, sort of.

But tonight, fuck it all. He was heading home to them now. Home. *Home.* Hopefully for the last time. Seriously. He didn't plan on leaving. Would do all he could to keep them safe and happen.

Okay, one detour through Utah first. No way around it. Dreaded every mile he drew closer.

He climbed out of the Olds, leaving it running, billowing out dark, rank exhaust, and walked around, leaned against the rear panel. He hoped anyone passing would think he was fixing a flat or taking a piss. Wished he could cross his arms. One big thing he still missed, not being able to cross his arms. He'd tried hugging his side-pork one-handed, but it felt weird. He shoved his hand into his jeans pocket, then crossed his ankles. James Dean pose.

He waited a while, not sure how long. Maybe fifty or sixty semi-truckloads, Slow Bear's eyes gritty from the dust they kicked up. He cleared his throat of diesel fumes. Still no sign of Lady, he walked out into the desert, dark as fuck, listening for her.

Followed her whimpers, gasps, and ragged breath, still enough light to make out her shape. Lady, on her knees, grasping her stomach, face inches from a quickly-absorbed pool of sick. He didn't say a word. The highway might as well've miles away.

The girl gagged, but had nothing left to puke. Nothing you

could smell or touch. More like regret, shame, whatever. Didn't matter how she was forced. The shame is from staying alive to take it when she could've taken another way out.

The fuck of it all, our will to live. Keep hoping tomorrow might be better despite all evidence to the contrary.

Might work for rich people. Hell, even the middle classes, sure. Why not?

The rest of the world? Bleak.

But each day is another day to eat, shit, fuck, listen to music, get drunk, get stoned, you know the drill.

From this distance, the semis on the highway sounded like Tie Fighters zipping across the surface of the Death Star.

Once the rope of drool connecting Lady to the dirt broke, she started breathing normally again. "I'm sorry. I'm real sorry. Please, I can't…"

"Yeah you can."

"I can't. I'm dying. Look at me, I'm dying, Micah."

"No you're not. Right now, your brain's telling you it's all my fault, but your body is the one you should listen to. Hold tight, ride it out, you'll feel better. Never great, but better."

"I want to fucking kill you right now."

Not going to push it. Let the Tie Fighters fill in the void, chase those fucking Rebels and their bullshit rag-tag army of farm boys. Worst case, she'd bolt somewhere down the road. Best, she'd stay put but try every trick the junk tells her to.

"This *sucks*! It sucks! Micah, goddamn you!"

"Mm hm."

Pew pew. Laser guns.

Lady sat up straight. Took in several deep but rough breaths. She put one foot beneath her, pushed up. Then the other. Slow motion. Hands on her hips.

They stood awhile, each staring off in different directions, wondering different things. Him, his girls in Nebraska, and Mama in Utah, no clue her daughter had passed, and Darwin and Lulu Belle in Californ-I-A, probably acting like it never happened, already ordering the next shipment of young ladies ready for the slave trade.

Lady, her next fix.

She moaned. Gave the moan some guts and probably spooked the prairie dogs out in the dark.

Slow Bear sighed. He got it. He understood perfectly.

"Kid."

She turned to him.

"Get in the fucking car already. We've got a long way to go."

Could be those would be his last words to her if she refused.

No, he wouldn't let her refuse. Not after coming so far. Not when he'd wasted two of his nine cursed lives already.

Thing was, she forced herself, with her dull-lidded eyes, and mouthbreather lips, to march to the car. Climbed in. Curled up and didn't say another word for the next fifty miles or so.

Slow Bear stopped at a gigantic truck stop, damn thing the size of a mall. He rented Lady a shower stall, let her clean up, while he found her a souvenir t-shirt and sweatpants, cheap flip flops, and a toothbrush and paste, and a small carton of Florida's Best to start her on the long road out of hell.

Chapter 21

By the time they pulled up to the curb outside Mama's place, the sun was high and merciless again, and Lady had finally slept after several more bouts of her needing to retch on the roadside. Each time was less horrible than the last, and she'd stopped begging Slow Bear for dope.

Of course she hadn't kicked it yet. Fuck no. Might never kick one hundred. But the wires in her head, as frayed and crackling with pain as they were, had stopped sparking quite so hard. Meant she could think sort of straight again. Still meant she was planning how to escape for her next fix.

Take it to the bank.

The harder he held on, though, the harder she'd fight to get loose. He kept his mouth shut unless it was important, drove in silence, without even the radio to keep him company.

Lack of sleep had him seeing gremlins all over the car, ripping it to pieces. Or in the rearview mirror, poking gremlin needles into Lady's ass. Or beside him in the passenger seat, asking if maybe getting Lady a fix wasn't the worse thing he could do. And a pop for himself, too, as a reward.

They burned away in the rising heat and dust of the morning.

So, Mama's house. Why not Cheetah's? After their wild visit from the cops, it would be a pretty good idea to steer clear of the condo for awhile. .

Mam's tank was in the driveway.

"Where are we?" Lady leaned forward between the seats.

"A stop I've got to make."

"Why?"

"The woman here is a friend of mine. Almost like a mother to me. I've got something to tell her."

Lady sank into the bench. "I'm going to stay here, maybe get a little more sleep."

Slow Bear opened the door. "Nope. Let's go."

He pulled the driver's seat forward and waited as Lady huffed and winced and bitched her way out of the car. The flip-flops were too big, as were the pants, tied with a drawstring nearly to her knees, but the shirt was too tight, exposing her stomach and pushing up her breasts. On her two feet, she squinted at the glare and grabbed hold of the trunk of the car to steady herself.

"Be nice," Slow Bear said.

Up the driveway, past the tank, to the kitchen door. He tugged the screen door, rapped his knuckles on the steel one.

Heard *I'm coming, I'm coming!*

Granting time for the older woman to hoist herself out of the recliner and get her knees straight before heading to greet them.

When Slow Bear heard her shuffling into the kitchen, he rapped again.

"Didn't I say I was coming? Hold your pants up."

She swung it open wide.

Her whole face brightened, dropped twenty years from her age. "The Prodigal returns! My my." Scanned his clothes, the shorts and shirt from the winery, as filthy as anything else he'd worn. "Looks like you've got a story to tell me."

Then she blinked at Lady, scrunched her eyebrows, and peered past the two visitors at her door. She leaned out the entryway, down the driveway. "Wait a minute."

Slow Bear cleared his throat. "She's not coming, Mama."

The woman lost the steel glint in her eye.

"Stop messing with me, boy."

Slow Bear laid his hand on her shoulder. "Listen…"

Mama jerked her shoulder from under his touch, stumbled across the kitchen, and slammed against the sink. Tight-lipped. A curt nod. "Y'all dropped her off in Provo, right? I bet. Needed alone time after this ruckus been going on. Up at Cheetah's, I bet. Shame, because I think the family is going to try to sell it out from under her. I mean, it's a nice place and all, but it's not worth…"

She ran out of breath.

Slow Bear ushered Lady inside. She glommed on to Slow Bear, turned her face away.

"No, I didn't drop her off. Maybe we should sit down and talk about it."

Mama sniffed and rolled her shoulders, held her arms wide to Lady. "She's your girl? The one you told me about? You found her? Young lady, if you only knew what our friend here has done to find you. Praise the Lord, praise the Lord, what'd Toni tell you? It was a Jesus thing after all."

Kylie didn't take the invitation for the hug. Murmured, "I never asked him to."

"Asked him to? Oh, sweetie. We don't have to ask for what we need. The Lord knows." She turned for the fridge, stepped over and opened it, pulled out a plank of chicken thighs. "I think you two need to stay for dinner. Let me throw something together."

"Please, no, you don't have to –"

"I *said* let me throw something together. You sit down and tell me all about it. Need to fry these things before they go to waste." Got her skillet from under the oven, filled it with canola oil.

"Mama, please. Talk to me."

"You're okay with spicy, right? It's one thing to put cayenne in the batter, but then I like to add a good dose of Dave's, too. The hot sauce, the insane sauce, he calls it. Makes everything a little, um, a little…*Jesus*!" She slammed the oil bottle on the counter. It fell over and spilled out onto the floor. Mama shook. "*Jesus! Lord, why? Why why why? You can't have her! You can't have her yet.*"

Slow Bear hurried to her side and escorted her into the living room, her TV still on but muted, Putin's face close-up, grinning. They zoomed out to show him shaking hands with Donald Trump.

He led her to the couch, sat beside her.

"I won't blame you, son, but I am *sorely* pissed at you right now. Watching me lose my religion like Job himself."

"It's killing me."

"How did she go? How did it happen?"

Slow Bear didn't want to tell her. Didn't want to remember. Saying those words would make it worse than the memory. Would lessen it somehow. He didn't want it to ever feel less than how it did right then. The sick feeling in his bowels. He'd carry it until another chance arose to destroy the bastards who'd done it.

"Bad men," Slow Bear said. "Real bad men."

He gave her the version he could stand to relive, which wasn't easy. Said it was quick, which it wasn't. Said it was merciful, which is wasn't.

"She was ready. Told me to tell you, see, I talked to her right before they, well, I talked to her and she told me to tell you she totally repented over liking girls."

It made Mama titter a little. Lips crawled up on the edges. "She was ready alright. Lying her butt off right before the Lord took her. I bet she didn't feel a thing. I bet Jesus pulled her soul a flash of a moment before Death's big ol' scythe got her. The only thing left was a hunk of meat."

"Fuck's sake, I hope so."

"Language."

Lady tiptoed in from the kitchen, not literally, but quiet as a dormouse, like the nursery rhymes said. Taking it all in. Absorbing. Slow Bear would tell her about it later on the way to Nebraska. At the moment though, she was lost.

But not thinking about getting high.

Mam sniffed again, took in a deep breath, and sat tall. Patted her hand on Slow Bear's knee. "You're about the worst Jesus thing ever happened to us."

"I wish Toni had never met me."

"Oh, shut your mouth. I didn't say Jesus things have to be pretty. Otherwise, they wouldn't be Jesus things. Toni's with Cheetah now, and you got your lady back. God's plan had some plot twists."

She stood and strode past them to the kitchen. "Help me clean up."

Chapter 22

They stayed the night – Mama insisted – and helped her clean the oil. She tossed a couple frozen pizzas in the oven for dinner instead of the chicken.

Slow Bear gave her more details on what happened to Toni, who was responsible, and why they'd never find her body. Probably fertilizing zinfandel vines.

Mama said, "Least it'll save me money on a funeral. Anyone asks, I'll tell them she went out West to find herself."

"He won't get away with it. I swear, I'm going back when I feel able. I'll burn him to the ground."

"Honey, you've done enough. It's okay. You done good."

"I can't help it. I can't."

"Well *try*. Stand down for now. You're owed a few, don't you think?"

Not the way he saw it. Not at all.

He slept on the couch while Lady took the guest room.

Well, "slept" was an overstatement. Not a wink.

Slow Bear thought he heard Lady sneaking out around three in the morning. He sat up, peered around, waiting for his eyes to adjust.

When they did, he checked the coffee table, where he'd tossed his crumpled cash and change.

It was still there.

Maybe he was imagining things.

Easiest thing to do would be get up, go peek inside her room.

He listened intently, thought he heard another person's breath, someone no good at stealth.

But Slow Bear didn't get up. The mere thought of having to

chase the girl down again, confront her, deflect all the abuse she would absolutely hurl at him – and with Mama for an audience, play it up even more – drained his resolve.

Okay, if she didn't want to go home.

Okay, if she wanted dope.

Okay, if she wanted to lash out.

None of it was easy. None of it even planned. He almost hadn't expected to find her. Now that he had, well, the odds of a Walt Disney ending retreated farther by the hour.

She deserved one. He didn't.

Truly goddamned sad.

Was she lurking n the shadows? Crawling along the wall? Trying hard to hold her breath until he settled again?

Finally, Slow Bear rose from the couch, fumbled his way towards the bathroom, and took a leak. Dark amber piss. He was dehydrated, squeezed out, his own body eating itself now.

He flushed, went to the couch, and laid down again.

Another glance at the coffee table.

His cash was gone.

Slow Bear would still be able to catch her if he went now. She was on foot, not familiar with the town, and probably not feeling her swiftest.

Then, the growl of the Olds engine he'd left on the curb. Didn't realize she knew how to start it with the wires. Maybe she's watched him do it, waiting for her moment.

Slow Bear laid his one-and-only hand on top of his head, grit his teeth to the breaking point, and held in a rage he was sure only fathers of murdered daughters shared.

Around seven in the morning, Slow Bear heard Mama begin to stir, humming under her breath, out of key, whatever key it was. A strained hum. He wondered if she'd lain in bed and stared at the ceiling, same as him.

Soon she appeared above him, arms crossed, eyes glassy.

"She gone?"

"Mm hm."

"Yeah."

She shook her head, then sat in her recliner and turned on the TV news. Loud as fuck.

Mama made biscuits while he showered. Crazy salty. She served them with Steen's Cane Syrup, thick like molasses, on the side. He dipped a biscuit in it and took a bite, a string of syrup dripping off his chin. Washed down by dark coffee stirred with honey and heavy whipping cream, turned tan.

They sat together at the kitchen table. She didn't eat or drink, watching him with her chin in her palm.

"You're welcome to stay with me, long as you need to. I'll make you work, make you pay for groceries, but at least you'll grow roots. Keep the house up."

"Sounds good. It sounds like a good offer."

"But what?"

Another bite of biscuit and syrup. Chewed slow.

"I've got a place to go already. I've got a woman waiting for me, still, I hope. Got two little girls she'll need help raising."

"Yes, you do. I understand."

"I'll call you, though. Love to have you join us. My casa, your casa, you know."

"Let's wait and see. Something tells me I wouldn't take to starting over again. But you promise to call, and we'll see. It's hard to beat the weather out here. Snow ain't good for my bones."

"What're you going to do?"

She gripped his hand with both of hers. "I've got friends. I've got cable. I've still got my driver's license. You let me worry about me. You get on to your people. They deserve to see you."

He walked down the driveway to the Olds, opened the door and caught a glimpse of something – *someone* – in the back seat.

She was curled into a fetal position, arms hugging her body.

Snoring.

If she'd scored, he couldn't tell. Didn't matter. Here she was.

Lady.

Slow Bear wanted to collapse. Not what he'd expected at all.

He stayed up, though. Swung the door wide, thumped down into the seat, and slammed it shut.

Lady jolted, but relaxed when she saw who it was. Pushed herself up, stared at her hands.

"Mama's got biscuits, if you're hungry."

She shook her head and rubbed at grouchy lines on her face.

"Ready to go?"

They met eyes in the rearview, and Lady about to launch into something. Excuses, bitching, petulance, whatever. Anything but an apology.

What she must've seen in Slow Bear stopped her cold.

What he was trying to say without saying it: *It's not worth talking about.*

No scolding, no begging. Moving on.

She closed her lips. Nodded.

He reached under the steering column and got the thing started again. Put it in reverse.

"Wait," she said.

Slow Bear braked.

"I think I do want a biscuit."

They parked and went inside.

Chapter 23

Twelve more hours on the road, Salt Lake City to Worms, Nebraska. Slow Bear was determined to make it straight through, not wanting to risk being hounded by cops or tracked by traffickers. He had no clue what he'd left behind, or if he'd become Public Enemy No. 1 in the wake of the motel slaughter. He had no clue what was ahead, either, after Darwin had suggested he knew more about the whereabouts of Abeline and the girls than Slow Bear thought he should.

His stomach cramped as he made the turn across the railroad tracks to Abeline's neighborhood. It was sparse, like the beginning of a development before it ran out of dough. The empty lots were now overgrown prairie grass and wind-strewn trash, the handful of houses surrounded by soybean fields.

Clammy palms on the wheel.

Tight throat.

"Jesus, what a dump," Lady said.

"Worse than the rez?"

"Worse than my side of the rez. You lived out in snake country."

True. He'd parked his Richardson Bi-Level trailer as far away from people as he could while staying on the reservation. No light pollution. The whole universe putting on a show for him. Not a dump. Heaven.

"Who is she? Your girlfriend?"

He shrugged. "She's no girl."

"She'd better be incredible if she's keeping you from fucking me."

Gave her a hard side-eye. "It's not her."

"Whatever." She pulled her hoodie over her head, crossed her arms, and pouted.

One more left turn. Bahamas Avenue. All the roads around here had been named for Caribbean getaways – Bahamas, Jamaica, Key West, Cozumel.

It was a funny joke. Probably what the contractors were thinking. Putting up gray-beige ranch homes, cookie-cutter, side-by-side while the wind smelled of cowshit and soybean processors, on a road called Bahamas.

There it was.

Nothing special about it except Slow Bear knew what was waiting inside. The trafficker's Suburban Abeline had escaped Utah in was parked in the driveway with Nebraska plates, all of the GPS hoo-ha scrambled by his hacker friend Owen. An empty flowerbed lined the front patio, a couple of old chairs rusting away, off to the side. Streaked with cobwebs.

What Slow Bear had hoped was he'd pull up to a vibrant home, rejuvenated. Last he was here, it was early Spring with snow on the ground. Now, he'd hoped for flowers, startling colors, a pair of girls' bikes. Anything.

He swallowed hard and got out, held the seat forward for Lady. Up the walk to the front door.

Before he reached his finger for the doorbell, the door opened and there was a pistol in his face.

It was held in both hands by a preteen girl. Pia was cleaner than last time, healthier all around, filling out. But her face – dark, snarling, tear-streaked.

She yelled, "Where the *fuck* have you been?"

Chapter 24

Slow Bear didn't flinch. He wondered if Pia could even squeeze the trigger of Abeline's .357 revolver with a six-inch barrel. She could barely hold it up.

Her arms started to the shake, and the weight of it was too much. Slow Bear caught the revolver before it hit the ground. He got down on one knee. Tried to embrace her.

She shouted and pounded her fists on him. "No! It's no fair! You left us! You were supposed to be here! It wouldn't have happened if you'd been here!"

But the effort wore her down and she dropped into his arm, crying.

Down the hall, Melody's face peeped from the backside of Abeline's bedroom door.

"What happened? Are you okay? You and Melody?"

Muffled into his shoulder. "You shouldn't have left us."

"I couldn't help it. I never meant to. What's happened?"

Melody started down the hall towards the door, her hair braided, new dress and sneakers, rosy-cheeked. Shyer than Pia, she stood out of reach, nowhere near as full of ire as her older foster sister.

A profound difference in both girls already. They'd been too small for their ages, dirty, barely clothed. Slow Bear had found them in Gerardo's Escalade. The bastard trafficker who was supposed to take them to Utah, then pass them along to other vermin for the next leg of the trip. This sick underground railroad of sex trafficking crisscrossing the States hundreds of times a day, preying on girls who'd either run out of options or weren't given the choice anyway.

Not these two. Not anymore.

Then he thought, *who's not here?*

"Where's Abeline? Is she here?"

Melody nodded.

He stood again, Pia still clinging to him. "Where is she?"

Melody pointed towards the end of the hallway, Abeline's bedroom. Slow Bear followed, having to nearly drag Pia, with Lady close behind. It was hot in the house, but Slow Bear had goosebumps. At the bedroom door, Pia let go. Melody stood at the foot of the bed.

The odor hit him first, strong. Someone who hadn't bathed in, what, days? Weeks?

Then the wheezing of an oxygen nebulizer. It sat at bedside, the size of an old fashioned vacuum cleaner. The tube snaked into the bed, under a thick layer of quilts over a comforter over the sheets, to a figure lying on its side. Slow Bear walked to the other side of the bed, knelt down, and pulled down the sheet covering most of the woman's head.

Not the redhead he remembered. She was going silver, with a few inches of dark brown left. The oxygen tube fit under her nose, her face lopsided. Left eye crunched up, left cheek and lips drooping, a pool of drool on the pillowcase. Like she'd aged twenty years.

But the spark in Abeline's good eye was still lit. She tried to smile.

Pia came around behind Slow Bear, said a bit too slow, a bit too loud, "It's Micah! Micah's here, can you see? It's MI-CAH!"

Her voice at first was a hiss, then a moan. Then, slurred but unmistakably, she whispered, "Where the *fuck* have you been?"

A half-hour later, Slow Bear sat on the edge of Abeline's couch, knees wide, elbow on one, head in hand.

He'd been thinking about this day for a while now, finishing his business out West and coming home scot free to his jury-rigged family. Finally here, it had all turned to shit. The worst kind of shit – explosive diarrhea. The bad news never stopped flowing.

Family. Unreal. After Slow Bear had lost his arm, he wanted to disappear, shrink away from everyone, sit on top of his trailer and feel sorry for himself. Not even drunk or high. He kicked heroin for the sole purpose of sulking in his right mind. But then all this, all *this*.

Never would've crusaded against sex traffickers if not for Lady being stolen away.

Never would've faked his death, wipe the slate clean, in order to murder these motherfuckers without too many prying eyes identifying him.

Never would've ever would've *ever* wanted a family to tie him down.

But…

Abeline was supposed to have been a one-night stand. Another in a line of drunk, lonely women lingering late at whatever dive bar he'd found at the end of each day as he tried to follow the traffickers who'd ripped Lady away from him from North Dakota to their final destination. Slow Bear had no money for hotels, and a few nights in Lady's tiny car, no backseat anymore, was enough to convince him there *had* to be better places to sleep.

Cozy up to a woman at the bar losing hope as closing time neared.

Nurse a Michelob for hours, keeping a clear head.

Find things they had in common. Music? Movies? Politics? Not like it would get heavy. Don't want to scare her off. Don't want her thinking you're a serial killer.

Hint around you'd like to spend the night with her. See her naked. Hold her close. Fat, acne-scarred, plain jane, or, you know, unfortunate in the body and face department. But hey, they deserved kindness. They had to be thinking the same thing, right? A one-armed, Indian with a face only a mother could punch, but a nice guy. As far as she could tell through the beer-goggle haze.

She'd invite him home. They'd fuck as long as they could stand it, then sleep til noon. Sit in the kitchen, drink coffee while she smokes a cig. Have a few laughs, give her a kiss good-bye, and trek on down the road.

That's what Abeline was supposed to be, a free bed and easy company. Slow Bear had to admit, even though she was twenty years older than him, plus a few, and she had a weathered shell from hard knocks, booze, smoke, and stress, Abeline had it going on. Sarcastic, a great tequila-stained laugh, and her deep red hair – dye, he found out later, but so what – and really fucking great in the sheets.

Still, he would've left her behind like the others if it hadn't been for finding the girls. They needed a place to go, and hers was the only place he could pull out of his brain on short notice.

She took them in. In her typically belligerent way, sure, but she did.

Abeline rode shotgun the whole way. Through a shootout in a Carl's Jr., through an ambush at a hotel, through being dragged to a trafficker's McMansion, minutes away from being murdered, through an inferno.

She stuck with him until he made her leave.

But damned if he wasn't going to see her again.

Here he was.

Devastated.

Earlier, Lady had started talking to the girls, a natural. She distracted them – "Show me your room. Can I paint your nails?" – while Slow Bear spoke with Abeline. He helped prop heron pillows, sat beside her.

"You got him? You really, um, you got him?"

He nodded. "Dead as fuck."

She laughed. It turned into a cough. She reached for him. Her good hand grasped his only hand. He leaned in, rested his cheek on hers.

"Why did it take…so long?"

"Too long. Couldn't help it."

"It's…been hard, Micah. Real hard."

"What happened?"

She told him it was a stroke. Two weeks ago? One week? Time was bullshit, couldn't remember. And since her own kids were up in arms about the new kids, her daughter getting the lawyer she was fucking under her husband's nose to send threat after threat, even though the records she'd gotten through Owen were rock solid…

"Forgotten how *hard* it is to raise girls. Pia hated me. Melody is…she bites. Quiet, but she'll bite."

"I should've come with you. I shouldn't have let you leave alone."

She shook her head. Might've rolled her eyes, he couldn't tell.

"Nonsense. Thought you…were dead."

"I could've –"

"Fuck…off. Now you're here. *Here*. Are you gonna stay?"

"Yeah, no, yeah, I'm not going anywhere."

He told her about finding Lady, about Darwin, about Toni and her mom. About how the next step up after Darwin was somebody named "Mr. Wall," the guy over the hotel operation. About him deciding he was done with his ridiculous crusade to come here instead.

"Helluva homecoming. I'm not…even wearing make-up."

"Who needs make-up? Don't worry. I'll take you to the hospital, get you in shape soon enough."

Abeline shook her head. Like one of those Hepburn women. The shaky one. "You…can't. You just…*can't*. What'll happen to…them?"

"You work on getting well, I'll make sure the girls are okay."

"Damn it, mother…*fucker*. Listen. It's not…not that easy."

He was exhausting her, the last thing he wanted to do. They'd have to talk about it later. He thought he'd left them in good hands. Abeline was a tank. A tiny one, but still. Now the tank was stuck in the mud and rusted.

Later, on her couch, staring at the floor, he tried to figure out the next step.

Pia walked in and sat beside him. Freshly painted toenails.

She said, "Kylie told us what happened to you."

"You mean the arm?"

"No, like, why you couldn't come with us. Why you were gone so long."

"Really? What'd she say?"

"You saved her, but all you could talk about was coming home to us."

Slow Bear turned to her. He hoped her face would stay young forever, and her eyes would shed the years they shouldn't have to carry. "I had to make a choice, remember? Help you and Abeline get away faster, or try to save myself. I chose you guys."

"We could've helped you."

"I know it. But if someone had got in our way, and I couldn't protect you…" Cleared his throat. "Things are going to be better now. You started school? You like it?"

"We haven't been in weeks. When they call, Abeline tells them we're sick, but she's the sick one."

"Then why didn't you call nine-one-one?"

Looked up at him like he was an idiot. "They'd take us."

"Who?"

"Her daughter, first. They'd split us up. The bitch would take Melody and sign up for benefit checks, Abeline said. And leave me with her son, which she said wasn't a good idea at all."

Slow Bear made a mental note to put him on the list.

"She tells me she's getting better, and tries to fake it. But I can tell, it's worse. And I've been worrying, like, what if she doesn't get better? What then?"

Wished he could wrap his arms around her and tell her it would all be peachy. But he was one arm short. "I'm going to think on it. We'll come up with something. Abeline will get better now. I'm here. I promise."

"I know." She glanced at the TV. "Can we watch TV now?"

"Go for it."

Melody must've been hiding around the corner, because as soon as Pia clicked the remote, the younger one came in as if she hadn't been listening. They plopped on their bellies, chins on hands, legs up and crossed. The way kids do. On the screen, one of the loudest and most ugly cartoons Slow Bear had ever seen. Nothing vulgar, except it was. Plump people, bucktoothed, red-faced. Spittle flying from shouting mouths, Jesus. Abstract backgrounds, like a Dali-thing going on.

Until Slow Bear recognized a couple of characters. Mickey Mouse. Pluto.

What? Since when had Disney decided to openly mind-fuck kids?

He shook it off, stood from the couch. Groaned. Too much pain sitting still. He'd need to get used to sitting. Staying still. Chores around the house, yeah, taking care of Abeline, yeah, going shopping, taking the girls to school, daily shit, yeah. But more time to *sit* and *be*. He didn't seem to have much *being* left in him. He'd chewed the world in bear-sized bites until it got too hard to keep chewing and turned around, empty-jawed, retreating to his cave. Abeline's cave.

Who was he if he wasn't killing motherfuckers?

Because it sure as shit wasn't who he was before he died from Santana's hotshot of heroin. Or the second time he died, or made everyone think he was dead, before heading out to recover Kylie, leaving bodies like roadkill in his wake. Or the third time, in the basement of a human trafficker, inhaling more smoke than a body should be able to, when an EMT only doing her job got an elbow from Jesus telling her Slow Bear was worth hardship.

Melody glanced over her shoulder at him. Only a few seconds, not a smile, not a frown, but not blank, either. A look saying she wasn't worried about him leaving or dying. A look to assure herself, *He's here, and I can watch cartoons and forget being scared for a while.*

How a normal kid might look at her normal stepdad.

Slow Bear left them watching cartoons while shut himself inside the bathroom, and balled up in the corner by the toilet. Determined to hold in whatever screams he wanted to let loose.

Might've busted some blood vessels in his eyes doing it, but by fuck, he did it.

Chapter 25

They came after dinner, delivery pizza boxes scattered around, all three girls in front of the TV again, a reality show about real housewives. Slow Bear had stayed in the kitchen. A pizza and a half down his gullet.

The cops.

Knocked on the door with their flashlights. Dicks. Can't even kiss their mothers without being intimidating.

Thud thud thud.

One of the pair shined his light into the front windows, even though the lights were on, TV on. Tapped the glass.

Pia and Melody froze in place. Too terrified to make noise, even. Kylie whispered to them, "It's okay, it's all okay."

Slow Bear eased through the kitchen, closer to the front.

Lady opened the door. "Hello? Everything okay?"

"Yeah, hon, we're looking for Abeline." A muffled, brusque man's voice.

Dude's partner was still pacing the front windows. Both wearing N95 masks.

"Yes it is. Something wrong?"

"Is Abeline here?"

Piece of shit. Poking, poking, poking. All he needed to say was what Slow Bear guessed they were here for: a wellness check called in by Abeline's kids. Trying to get their inheritance – the few cents in the couch cushions it might be. They didn't care about their mom's health. They wanted her in a hospital bed tied to tubes feeding her sedatives, controlling her.

Were the cops authorized to actually remove the kids right here and now?

Was Slow Bear going to let them?

He sneaked across the floor to the kitchen drawers, opened them painstakingly slow. What did he have to work with?

A meat mallet.

Worked before, might work again.

"Miss, who are you?"

"I'm Kylie, her babysitter? I've been helping out while she's got Covid."

The partner cop had moved around to the side of the house now, beam shining through the kitchen window. Slow Bear dropped into a crouch. Hoped the light hadn't caught his shadow.

A meat mallet. Two cops and a meat mallet.

Because he was too mad to use Abeline's gun.

"You're saying Abeline has Covid?"

"I'm sorry, what's going on?"

"Can we come in?"

"I don't…why would you…?"

The screen door screeched open, whapped against the cop's backside.

"Sweetie, we need to check on Miss Abeline. Her daughter's worried about her. Hasn't heard from her in days."

"I don't know anything about it."

"But you're the babysitter? For?"

"Her adopted girls. Do you mind stepping back? We've kept the girls out of school to keep them safe. I don't want to risk anything."

The meat mallet.

Slow Bear lifted it, gripped it hard. His mouth went dry.

Couldn't even make it through one goddamn night of pizza and shit TV.

"I'm going to have to ask you to step outside."

"But, the girls –"

"Please."

Slow Bear inched forward, the door blocking him from the cops. Kylie's eyes flicked after him and he clenched his jaw hoping the cop wouldn't catch it.

"Is someone else with you, other than the girls and Miss Abeline?"

Fu-uh-uh-uhck.

He'd been a cop on the rez. His brothers in blue (they never wore blue) had kicked him out, tossed him aside like a half-smoked cigarette. Didn't mean he wanted to start killing cops. Jesus. Is this what "family" means? Killing fucking cops, guys doing their jobs, to protect your wife, kids, nieces, nephews, whoever else?

Yeah, probably.

Two at once with a meat mallet.

Shit odds.

A rough shout from down the hall. "Who's there? Kylie, sweetie, who's at the door?"

Abeline's voice. Slow Bear leaned a little further, caught a glimpse of a zombie woman bracing the wall, trudging forward. Sweatpants and a t-shirt swallowed her whole.

Slow Bear waited in the shadows.

"Who is it?"

"Police, Miss Abeline. I told them not to come in, because of the girls."

"Let the man in. Jesus, let him in. The girls will be fine. Kids bounce back. Let the man in."

Her voice, still slurry, but less so. She was fighting Hell itself to stand in the hallway pretending to be fine. Even her stroke-numbed face seemed healed for the moment. A miracle.

The cop at the door called for his partner. Slow Bear was trapped now. He could listen, but couldn't see what was happening.

The radio buzz and clanking of the cops' tools belts, loaded to the hilt, drew closer, with both cops stepping inside.

Abeline cleared her throat. "Kylie, sweetie, get me a mask."

"No ma'am, not necessary."

"You don't want this mess, the virus. Goddamn Chinese." She coughed. Wheezed.

"You have Covid?"

"Probably. Who knows? What are they going to do? Tell me I

do then send me home? Or hook me up to one of…one of…what's the breather, the machine?"

"Respirator?"

"From what I hear, the machine is the thing that kills you. People go in, got a cold, they get hooked up to the respirator, boom. The end."

"Are you sure you don't want a doctor? We could take you to the hospital."

"Aw, sweet of you boys." She let out a ragged cough like a pick scraping guitar strings. "You think I'm sick now, should've seen me…whoa, like four days ago. What day is it? I mean, I couldn't get out of bed. I couldn't lift my arm. See, still can't."

The second cop spoke low to his partner, something like, "Looks like a stroke to me."

The first cop hummed *Mm-hm.* "Your daughter hasn't heard from you lately. Asked us to stop in, check on you."

"Good lord. I'll text her. I'll text her right now."

"Ma'am, are you sure it's Covid?"

"You already asked me. What did I tell you?"

"I mean, are you sure it's not something else? Like a stroke?"

Something like laughing, if you bent your head right. "I've seen men with strokes. I know all about them. Boys, please. I'm on the mend. I'll get some medicine, what's it called? inver… IVERmeltin, something, right?"

"No, ma'am, I don't think it works."

"You sure? The President said it works."

The cops exchanged shorthand between radio blips, Slow Bear picking up *She's fine* and *None of our business* and *Bitch wasting our time.*

A couple minutes and a handful of coughs from Abeline later, the first cop said, "Please, ma'am, call your daughter. She's really worried about you."

"I'll tell you, she's more worried about selling my house when I'm dead and gone. Bet she'd rather you guys tell her I'm dead."

"Well, you two will have to work out. I hope you feel better soon."

"You boys be safe."

They clanked and buzzed outside. Kylie eased the door closed, leaned against it, eyes wide.

She whispered, "You were amazing."

Slow Bear stepped into the hall, crouched low in case the cops decided to peek through the windows. Abeline, grinning, the wall holding her up, with the girls standing in the door of their bedroom behind her, was quite a sight.

"Look at you."

She shook her head. "We can't…we can't let that happen again."

The heavy slur had returned.

"I know."

She placed her hand on her hip and caught her breath. "You're going to have to marry me."

Kylie's breath caught.

Funny enough, Slow Bear had thought the same thing standing in her kitchen, listening to her handle those cops like she was on steroids. Marry her, adopt the girls, and make sure Abeline's kids were left out in the cold. Hell, Kylie could stay, too, if she could keep clean.

Slow Bear went to one knee, wobbled, but held on. "Yeah, babe. Yeah, I will."

Abeline let out a breath. "Well, thank the devil. Got my hooks in you."

Her head lolled and she began to collapse like a house of bricks. Pia yelped. Slow Bear lunged, caught Abeline under one arm and eased her to the carpet.

"Hey, babe? You okay?" He held his hand to her chest. Her heart was beating. She blinked and reached for him. "You okay?"

"I'm tired, lover. Please, take me to bed."

Slow Bear and Kylie helped Abeline to her feet. If he'd had two arms, he would've scooped her up in both. With only one, he hefted her over his shoulder like a sack of potatoes.

"Lady, help the girls to bed. Stay with them."

The bartender looked young again. Too young. Scared.

"Micah…"

"We need you tonight, okay? They need you."

She nodded. Shivering.

"Come get me if you need me."

He carried Abeline to her bedroom. Closed the door.

She chuckled, low. "Carrying me across the threshold."

"Yeah."

"Like a caveman."

He eased her onto the bed.

"Please, Micah, these clothes. I'm burning up."

He helped her with the t-shirt. The skin underneath pale, mottled. Hair thick under her armpits. Tits sagging. She smelled like an egg salad left in the sun. Slow Bear didn't care. Tomorrow he'd carry her to the bath and spruce her up again. Next, her sweatpants. Gently, gently. Her blue underwear, a wet spot. She'd pissed herself from the effort of standing up to those cops. He took those off, too, asked if she wanted to wear something else.

"I want goosebumps. I want a cool breeze."

Slow Bear switched off the space heater and turned on the oscillating fan in the corner. It didn't move much air, but each time it passed, Abeline let out a satisfied moan. He forced open the weather-sealed window, Abeline too busy to strip the silicone from winter. The heat whooshed past into the outside air.

Slow Bear turned out the bedroom light, sat on the empty side of the bed. Kicked his boots off, his socks. short, underwear. The awful Fiskadoro shirt. Abeline was right. The sun was warm on his skin. A relief. It made him forget about his situation for the moment. Turned down the heartburn. The literal heartburn. The fire inside he hadn't been able to shake since hearing those sons of bitches kill Toni.

The fire inside had burned years off his life already. He could tell. He'd never expected to live forever, but now he wished he could tack a few more on for Abeline's sake. The girls' sakes.

"Micah?"

He slipped under the sheets, spooned her. Feeling her against him again after thinking he might never again, even in her current state, he couldn't help but grow hard.

Abeline said, "Goddamn, boy, I was about to ask if you were

having second thoughts, getting chained to an old bitty like me."

He squeezed her. "Sorry."

"Hell, sorry for what?"

"For not coming sooner."

"Came as soon as you could. You found your girl. Something good to come out of it all."

"I hope. She's a junkie now."

A broken sigh. "Nobody's perfect."

"The girls come first. If it means Kylie has to go, she has to go."

"You're a hard man."

"Hm."

He kissed her neck. She flinched and giggled, ticklish. Flashback to their first night together, the only night he'd expected to spend here. Drunken, sloppy, desperate fucking. Two people who'd only known each other a couple hours. Abeline had been surprised he wanted to go home with her, young buck like him, handsome even with only one arm. She didn't have the clearest memory of the night, but he did.

"Why me?" She'd asked much later.

"I liked your voice. I liked your hair. I liked your lipstick."

Now, the room finally chilling down, a sheen of sweat between them, Abeline said, "If you want to, you can. I'll let you."

"What?"

"Give it to me. Fuck me. *Make love*, whatever. I'd love for you to."

Slow Bear squeezed her. Another kiss on her neck, his lips lingering. "Wait until you're better. I don't want to risk anything."

"Risk what? I'ma lay here and smile at you, call you a dirty Indian. You owe me."

"Abeline."

"Your cock on my ass says otherwise. Might as well."

He was about to make an excuse, say he was exhausted, or the girls might hear, or, or…or what?

He whipped the sheet off. Abeline flopped onto her back. Her pale skin, almost glowing. She spread her legs and he eased between them, always a challenge to hold himself too long on a single arm.

She reached for him, slicked him with his own pre-cum. She was already wet, either with sweat or desire, he'd only find out as he pushed into her.

Desire.

"Oh, fuck, that feels good."

Yeah, he had to admit, it really did.

She flexed hard to hold him tight as she could. It wasn't much, but he liked it. Being here again, feeling her again, *fuck*.

He didn't last long.

Collapsed onto her. When he tried to move, thinking he was too heavy, she grabbed behind his neck and held him down.

"Where you going?"

"Don't want to crush you."

"Not the worst way to go."

Slow Bear kept his tears in check, son of a bitch, but it hurt. After a while, he got up, spread the sheet over Abeline, and climbed in beside her again. She was already asleep, breathing steady. He closed his eyes. The days and weeks pressed down on his brain, and forced him into a grave of sleep. Deeper than deep. Not even existing.

Three-o-six AM.

Something jarred him awake. He held his breath and listened. Had they found him? Sooner than he'd expected. He'd even left the window open all night. Jesus. Listened harder, not wanting to disturb Abeline.

But he heard nothing.

The front door? Kylie sneaking out?

No, not tonight.

Nothing. Silence. Hard, dark silence.

Which was when Slow Bear knew. Not a noise, but a lack of one.

Abeline's steady breath.

It wasn't there anymore.

Chapter 26

Dead dark when he slipped out of Abeline's bedroom.

CPR hadn't worked. How long? Ten, twenty minutes? How many broken ribs? One-handed? Fuck!

Calling Kylie to help would've woken the girls. Not how he wanted them to remember Abeline.

He spied on them, Pia sprawled across her bed on top of the blanket, while Kylie and Melody huddled tight on hers, comforter pulled up to their cheeks. Closed the door with nary a click.

The garage.

A shovel.

As much as he hated it, going through the normal channels was out of the question. Even if they were to clean the scene and bolt, making an anonymous call from somewhere else, it was too late. The cops from last night, Abeline's children, someone out here hooked into Wall's organization hearing about it on the news. Alarm sirens. A trail.

Slow Bear couldn't risk it.

The soybean fields behind the houses in Abeline's neighborhood stretched for miles, treeless except for windbreaks to protect the homes from inescapable mountains of snow piling against their walls, and from brutal summer winds and storms. Clumps of twisted cottonwoods, hackberry, the husks of ash trees decimated by insects.

He headed for a wide one separating the yard from the field, hidden from view, impossible to finish by sun-up. He struck the ground with the shovel, testing the hardness. Easier if he dug in the field to avoid tree roots, but, again, he'd be seen. Being seen equaled calling the cops. Calling the cops equaled…

As he tried to wedge the first shovelful of dirt from the ground, the gospel truth set in. A one-armed man was *not* going to dig a grave.

Not even a grave for a cat.

He tried, fucksake, he tried. Stabbing the dirt, slamming his boot heel into the shovelhead, wrenching out a measly divot, only to have most of it fall off in the same spot. Hardened, determined, he tried again. Again. Again. AGAIN.

Againagainagainagainagain.

Slow Bear dropped to his knees, palm full of splinters, blisters, blood oozing. A monster scream pulsing in his chest, but he held it, by God. He shook violently until he finally opened his mouth and exhaled and nearly passed out.

He moved to the soybean field, fuck the neighbors. Softer dirt between the rows of plants. But still, he couldn't keep the shovel steady enough to lift much soil without it falling to the side or back into the hole.

Forty minutes later, he was not even knee-deep.

He left the shovel in the hole and trudged towards the house. The dark was dissipating to gray. The wind fucked with his ears.

It was time to wake Kylie.

Chapter 27

They were on the road by eight in the morning. Kylie and the girls took Abeline's Suburban and headed west, carrying a letter addressed to the person at their destination. Slow Bear had written it himself. Took a damned long time, what with the state his hand was in. Kylie helped take out the splinters and wash it, then wrap it in gauze.

They didn't want to leave.

Slow Bear told them, "Abeline has got a lot sicker, and I'm going to need to take her for help. It's not safe for you to stay while we're gone. Trust me. Go on with Kylie, and we'll meet up with you later."

The lie making his throat ache.

Melody clung to his neck. Her face was a mess – tears, snot, confusion.

"Can I see Ms. Abeline? I want to tell her goodbye."

"Sorry, hon, she needs her rest. She wishes she could, though"

Pia exploded. "It's bullshit. I'm going with you and Abeline. You can't stop me."

"Watch me."

She launched from the chair and raced down the hall, about to open Abeline's bedroom door when Slow Bear overtook her, blocked the path. He led both girls to the living room, made them sit on the couch while he knelt in front of them.

He remembered finding the girls in Gerardo's SUV, a wave of exhaustion hitting him when he realized what was going on. He did what any sensible vigilante would do – tried to drop them with the last woman he'd slept with. Except she wasn't having it, then some thugs cruised down the street and clocked them because he'd driven Gerardo's sweet Cadillac Esplanade, which they'd obviously tracked.

Pia's face, God, how angry. Melody blinking tears.

"You saw what I did to the people who hurt you."

They nodded.

"Everything I do, *everything*, is to keep you both safe. Sometimes you've got to trust me and do what I tell you."

Kylie stepped in and took Melody by the hand. "Come on, let's get you packed. Let's pick which toys you want to bring."

When they'd gone into the girls' bedroom, Pia looked up at Slow Bear.

"She'd dead, isn't she?"

He let out a huff and rubbed his eyes. "Would it make a difference if I said yeah?"

Pia considered it. She was a hard one. No tears. Only righteous fucking pissed-offedness. Maybe she'd end up waging her own war against those motherfuckers, *Kill Bill* style. She screwed up her mouth like she was about to shout at him again, but instead deflated.

"I'm sorry," she said.

"S'okay."

They packed quickly, left quickly, Kylie doing a stellar job of keeping them occupied the whole time. A real heroic performance. Slow Bear hoped – fuck, *prayed* – she could keep off the junk, at least long enough to finish the trip.

Before climbing behind the wheel, Lady turned to him. "Talk to you soon?"

Knowing she wouldn't. The only thing keeping her together was the girls needing a steady hand. The strength in her, good to know it was welling up again.

"You know me. I'll be around."

"I'll make sure to have a pitcher orange juice waiting. Fresh-squeezed."

Time for a hug, a kiss, anything.

But they both stood bolted to the ground. Magnets repelling. After all he'd done to get her back.

Slow Bear lifted his hand, a half-assed wave. "Go on, now."

He watched them drive away.

Lumbered inside.

He found the t-shirt Abeline had been wearing the night they met. Brooks & Dunn. As difficult as it was, her limbs stiffening now, he dressed her in the shirt, her boot-cut jeans, and cowboy boots. He arranged her in the middle of the bed, hands clasped. The room was freezing – central air, oscillating fan and ceiling fan all going at once. Keep her as cold as possible.

He made sure the revolver was loaded, found more ammo on her closet shelves. He chose the biggest and best knives from the kitchen. Found more heavy tools and rust-cragged saw blades in the garage.

Slow Bear set about to *Home Alone* the joint.

Halfway through, exhausted and probably infected with tetanus, he gave up. It was no movie. No cameras, no audience. No reason.

So he sat. Planted himself in the living room Laz-E-Boy and waited.

Three days.

He finished the last of the food – Pop-Tarts and saltines, cans of Chunky Beef and Campbell's Cream of Mushroom, frozen chicken breasts, thawed then microwaved down to rubber. Tap water to drink.

Slow Bear checked Abeline's cell phone. Texted the daughter, as only Abeline could, *Fuck's sake, girl, it's just Covid. I've had worse. I'm taking the girls to Vegas with me and my new friend. He's putting us up at the Venetian, and I'm turning my goddamn phone off for the rest of the weekend!*

He took out the sim card, snapped it in two, and crushed the phone under his boot heel.

A week.

He filled gallon freezer bags with ice and surrounded Abeline with them. Even with the constant frigid air conditioning, the fan, and the ice, he couldn't stop the bloat. The green hue. The fluid leaks.

Slow Bear finally covered her with a thick plastic tarp from the garage, spotted with house paint all over. Tucked it in. He found a threadbare quilt in her closet, probably passed from daughter to granddaughter to great granddaughter, draped it over as well.

Dignified? Fuck no. No dignity at all. Too weak to dig her a grave, and not willing to get caught by the cops for calling someone to come pick her up and give her the decency she deserved.

Selfish? Fuck yes. But he couldn't imagine Abeline, alive or dead, wanting him to spend the rest of his life in prison. He'd be glad she was dead so's not to see it.

Fuck, he wasn't glad about anything. Devastated by her. His life had stopped along with hers. Having a hard time thinking of tomorrow and tomorrow and on except in the most primal way – the will to live propping him up. Something unconscious. Having been dead before, literally and figuratively, some force in his brain refused to let him end things the easy way. His lungs didn't want to starve for breath. His nerves didn't want to feel the pain of the blade or the bullet.

A purgatory of his own design.

Abeline's rotting corpse, no food, no one to save and no one to save him. Waiting for what he knew was coming, hoping he'd make it long enough to carry it through.

Two weeks.

The cops came by again. Another wellness check, but Slow Bear stayed statue-still behind the door. They said, *I don't think anyone's home*. They said, *Why doesn't her daughter drag her own lazy ass out here for once?* They said, *Maybe she got herself to the hospital.*

The cops left.

The power blinked out. The electric company shutting it down. No more air conditioning. No more fan.

Abeline's stench overpowered the house. Slow Bear suffered it, didn't run from it like his body wanted to. His lungs itched, wheezed. His eyes burned, red and watery. His stomach roiled. He puked until empty, then dry-heaved until he passed out.

What was he doing? Why?

Sometimes he'd find dead crickets in the kitchen, the

bathroom. He ate them.

It didn't help.

A month.

Slow Bear lost track of time, spending days at a stretch on the couch, awake but unaware. His mind giving up the fight. He had no reason to get up anymore. No food meant nothing to shit, nothing to puke. The smell faded, or he was getting used to it. He accepted it. Kind of like drowning. At some point, no matter how hard you fought or held your breath, you were going to inhale the water and understand your last breath was going to kill you.

He drank from the tap until the water company cut the flow. Supposed he'd only have a few more days to live once the water was gone. Still a little water in the toilet tank. Enough to get him through week eight.

Two months, four days.

They finally showed up.

Chapter 28

Late into the night, as he expected.

Slow Bear was sure they'd sent scouts to drive by, get the lay of the land ahead of time.

"Gauge the sitch," the kids would say.

The last two days, shadows, dark figures passed by the front windows. Once or twice, stopping to cup their hands together against the glass. He'd heard murmuring. Imagined it was, "What stinks?" or "I swear he's right there on the couch."

When the caravan of SUVs – of course they were SUVs, everyone drove SUVs anymore – pulled into the driveway and on the curb, Slow Bear woke to the real world. Weak, but not done. Adrenaline was a hell of a chemical. Vehicle doors opened, men poured out, doors closed. Slow Bear reached between the cushions, lifted Abeline's .357, and pushed himself off his tomb of a couch.

He limped down the hall, opened Abeline's bedroom door. A wave of nasty gas billowed into the hallway, nearly taking Slow Bear to his knees.

One last look.

Most would've run screaming. Gagged. Imprinted it onto their nightmares.

Slow Bear bent down and kissed her cheek.

When the first goon pried open the door into the laundry room, a circular saw with razor-sharp teeth tied to a stiff wire swung down and slammed into his face. If they'd been told to keep quiet, it didn't last long. The scream told Slow Bear his trap had done massive damage to his eye, nose, and teeth.

Maybe I should've set up more of those.

One down.

Fuck knew how many to go.

Couple other goons pulled their buddy out and rushed forward to the next doorway, crouched down, and sprayed the kitchen with AR-15s.

Slow Bear took it in. His eyes had adjusted to the dark after all those nights alone. The goons wore bulletproof vests and night vision goggles. He wondered if any of the trafficker's Satanic SWAT team here were real police officers moonlighting. Wouldn't surprise him. Some of those assholes with badges would shoot anyone for cash, didn't matter if it was on salary or under the table.

Once the kitchen was breached, the front door splintered off its hinges.

Flash bangs smashed windows. Thunder and lightning.

Slow Bear was prepared. Cotton in his ears, shades on his eyes.

Watching from the attic. Feeling gritty.

None of the…*one two three*…seven goons in the house had bothered to look up and notice the holes where air vents had been before.

Three of them approached Abeline's room, goddamn them. They entered, gagged at the odor, peeled off the quilt and tarp.

"Motherfucker!"

"What the *fuck*?"

"I'm gonna be sick."

Before the puny goon could dash out of the room, Slow Bear lit three Molotovs – Black Velvet bottles refilled with gasoline, Abeline's underwear shoved into the neck – and dropped them down on their heads.

Two of the bottles smashed on the floor and the flames spread like *Hell itself* across the floor, up the curtains, onto the bed, up the legs of the goons.

They screamed and lifted their guns, fired into the ceiling. Slow Bear had already darted to the other side of the house.

"He's in the attic! The fucking attic!"

Two of the gunmen fled from the bedroom, flames eating

their jeans, out the front yard to roll around, slap the inferno away. The last was too late, still firing until his clip emptied, the gun fused to his skin. He lost his way, bumping into walls, tripping onto the bed, struggling up and finally making it through the door, engulfed. "Get it off! Get it off!" He collapsed in the living room, throwing flames across the floor.

Slow Bear tossed a few more bottles into the living room, then the kitchen for good measure, the goons firing and fleeing at the same time.

Couldn't be too long before deputies started showing up. Not as quick as Lincoln or Omaha, not as quick as a suburb, but still. These guys had already risked too much, too long. They were goddamned *committed* to getting their man.

The flames leapt higher, up the walls, lighting the attic. The smoke rose, black and oily. Slow Bear covered his mouth with a wet washcloth – enough water left in the toilet tank – and skittered across plywood spread over the beams to the hole in the roof he'd cut through the day after the girls had left with Kylie.

He wondered if they were okay. If Kylie had made good on her promise.

No time for wonder. No time for doubt, either.

He struggled out the hole onto the roof. Reminded him of when he set his trailer ablaze on the rez. Except now he had no escape plan.

This fight was all he'd been waiting for. His will to live will have crossed the finish line if he could make sure another trafficker had been taken off the face of the Earth. Impossible to stop the bastards forever – new sickos sprouting all the time, new greed – but these ones, *these ones*, fuck them.

He duck-walked to the extension over the patio. He'd practiced the move, but long ago when he still had energy and muscle. Gun in his waistband, placed his hand on the edge of the shingles, jumped into space and turned. His fingers scraped against the shingles, not slowing his fall like he'd hoped.

Flailed. Landed on his side. On his arm.

Snap.

His pain center overloaded. Broken bone in his only arm. He sat up, shaking. Forced his broken arm to reach for the gun. Barely able to open and close his fingers. Not even sure he could fire the revolver, with its heavy trigger.

Something urged him on, though.

Something.

He found enough strength to stand and walk. Slow steps. He kept close to the house. The wall held him up as he made each step, cringing.

He rounded the front corner. The few remaining goons headed for the SUVs.

Again, *fuck them.*

Slow Bear lifted Abeline's revolver, the weight of it astounding now, and fired. Propelled forward by another surge of adrenaline, each shot sent jolts of electricity up his arm to his head.

He gunned down one of the goons, but it took at least three shots. No idea where the other three went.

He was done. Dropped the revolver. He had a couple fast-loaders in his pockets, but his arm had done its duty and fucked off, numb now.

The first volley of AR bullets smashed into his ribs, through at least one lung.

Down to his knees.

More whizzed by. One took off his left ear. Another couple in his stomach.

"Alive! I said alive! The fuck are you doing?"

A passenger in one of the SUVs clambered from his seat. Middle-aged, a little fat, Senator-style hair, wearing a flak jacket over an Oxford shirt and khakis. He started towards Slow Bear, his hands raised. "Stop! Stop shooting!"

Another slug ripped into Slow Bear's crotch – *of course it did*, he thought – and he fell to the ground, twisting onto his back.

The fire, wild now, pulsing waves of heat. Sirens in the air, but faint. The remaining goons surrounded him, glared at him, as their leader broke through the ranks, panting. He braced his hands on his knees, giving Slow Bear the once-over.

"You know who I am?"

Slow Bear took a stab. "Mr. Wall."

"Good guess. Sergio Wall. Not my real name, but dead or not, I'm not telling you my real name. I want you to realize, you never knew the truth. Never had a clue what you were really up against. You were a gnat is all you were."

Blood rose in Slow Bear's throat. He cleared it, coughed more out. Not long now.

Wall stabbed a finger at Slow Bear's face. "Micah Cross. Slow Bear. Obviously got the right guy, right?"

"Sure do. Sure as shit do."

"You fucked up a lot of my people. A *lot* of them. You stole my property."

"Sicko." Couldn't put sentences together anymore. His vision narrowed. "Pedo."

"Feels good to spend your dying words calling me names? I'll sleep like a baby tonight. Not a care in the world now you're a dead man. I wanted you alive. I wanted to take you with us and make you suffer one hour for every hundred thousand dollars you cost me." He stood straight, waved one of the goons over, one holding a plastic grocery bag, sagging like it was holding a ham. "I've got something for you."

The goon dumped the contents. Like two hams. But not hams. Heads. The wide-eyed, black and green heads of Darwin and his sister, Lulu Doll. They rolled inches away, Slow Bear's nose almost touching Lulu's lips.

"I guess I'm a winemaker now, too. You did me a favor. These idiots had it coming. Now why don't you tell me where you stashed my property so I can get out of here?"

Slow Bear thought about his last resort. The chef's knife. Up his sleeve, slicing his skin, ready for him to work it out into his palm and slam it into Wall's jugular. He tried to speak.

"What?"

Slow Bear coughed more blood, dragged in a harsh breath. Smoke. Burning flesh. "Closer."

Wall knelt beside him.

Slow Bear flexed his wrist, like he'd practiced, to work the blade from his sleeve to his hand. Easy, easy. Only one shot.

Wall leaned as close as he was going to get. "What're you saying?"

Now.

Slow Bear tried to lift his arm but it didn't. Tried again. Nothing.

Once more. A tremor. A pulse of nerves.

Nothing.

"Are we done here? Done fooling around? I'm going to find them, you know. I'm going to get my money's worth."

Slow Bear's lips turned up. A grin. Cleared his throat again, made sure he had enough breath left to say, "Ain't life a bitch?"

Wall stood, shook his head. "Shame. Wish you'd lived to watch me win, Mr. Cross, or Mr. Bear, or whatever your name is."

Maybe he said it too low for them to hear. Maybe he imagined it.

Telling the piece of shit, "Call me No Bear."

Wall walked back to SUV. "Shoot him in the head and let's go."

It came down to a nameless, bearded white-boy goon out playing mercenary. No one special, no grand sacrifice. He glared down at Slow Bear with pity. "Asshole."

The barrel hovered over his forehead.

And just that quickly…

EPILOGUE

Mama,

I couldn't risk calling. They're everywhere. They're going to find me soon. They're coming after these girls, too, and they'll find them. But I know, with you, they'll be safe.

Sorry if I'm asking too much of you, but like Toni always said, 'It's a Jesus thing.' You already know Kylie, and she needs a strong hand to set her straight again. It wasn't her fault. She's got a good heart, but she's going to break yours like she has mine. Don't give up on her.

The girls' names are Pia, the older one, and Melody, the younger. They've been through Hell on Earth like you wouldn't believe, and since I can't be there to protect them anymore, I'm trusting you to, more than anyone I could think of. Please, when it gets tough and you think you can't keep going, remember, Toni died for these two. Not for me, but for them.

I guess that's all I can think to tell you. You'll figure out the rest, I know you will. An honor to know you,

Micah

PS – Don't worry about me. If you're reading this, I'm dead and in a very special place in Hell for bad men who tried to do the right thing. I got what was coming to me.

Acknowledgements

- Brandy, always there, always encouraging, always keeping my chin up. Much love. She's also the one who started the "Slow, Slower, Slowest" thing.
- Chris McVeigh and Christopher Black for holding on with me through these weird little novellas. Fahrenheit has been a wonderful home for Slow Bear.
- My colleagues at Southwest Minnesota State University's English and Creative Writing Program, who think it's cool I write about awful people doing awful things.
- My closest buds, Victor Gischler and Sean Doolittle, who have talked me off ledges and helped bring me up from the depths many times over the past twenty-plus years. Always grateful.

About the author

Anthony Neil Smith is the author of numerous crime novels, short stories, and essays. He is an English Professor at Southwest Minnesota State University.

He likes British beer, Mexican food, and Italian crime flicks from the 70s. His newly adopted dog is named Edmund, and he is the devil.

You can find out more about his work on his website

www.anthonyneilsmith.com

By the same author.

- *Slow Bear*
- *Slower Bear*
- *The Butcher's Prayer*
- *Trash Pandas*

More books from Fahrenheit Press

Know Me From Smoke by Matt Phillips

Stella Radney, longtime lounge singer, still has a bullet lodged in her hip from the night when a rain of gunfire killed her husband. That was twenty years ago and it's a surprise when the unsolved murder is reopened after the district attorney discovers new evidence.

Royal Atkins is a convicted killer who just got out of prison on a legal technicality. At first, he's thinking he'll play it straight. Doesn't take long before that plan turns to smoke—was it ever really an option?

When Stella and Royal meet one night, they're drawn to each other. But Royal has a secret. How long before Stella discovers that the man she's falling for isn't who he seems?

"A beautifully written, brutal & brilliant slice of hardboiled crime fiction. A Knockout."

Pure by Jo Perry

Caught in a pincer movement between the sudden death of Evelyn (her favourite aunt) and the Corona virus, Ascher Lieb finds herself unexpectedly locked down in her aunt's retirement community with only Evelyn's grief-stricken dog Freddie for company.

As the world tumbles down into a pandemic shaped rabbit-hole Ascher is wracked with guilt that her aunt was buried without the Jewish burial rights of purification. In order to atone for this dereliction of familial duty, Ascher – in her own words 'a profane, unobservant, atheist Jew, frequent liar and grieving loser' –volunteers to become the newest member of Valley Haverim Chevra Kadisha, a Jewish burial society on-call twenty-four-seven during lockdown and performing Mitzvot at no cost to the bereaved.

What follows is a journey through the insanity of lockdown in

Los Angeles as Ascher attempts to bring peace to a troubled soul, and perhaps in the end redemption for herself.

"The mystery will get under your skin, for sure, but the humanity of this novel will resonate far beyond the page."

Red Honey by Saira Viola

Red Honey is the much-anticipated new book from the hugely critically acclaimed Saira Viola.

With an introduction from Todd Robins, editor of Vautrin Magazine, Red Honey is a collection of never before published short stories & flash fiction from a recognised giant of the genre - to say people are excited about this book is the biggest understatement of the year.

"Saira's prose seeps from the page, through the senses and into the soul without appearing to trouble the brain. In a way, that wide-screen, surround-sound experience of reading her work is a double edge sword. It's like watching a firework display; the pretty sparks falling all around can make you forget it was born of gunpowder." - Russell Day, Author of King Of The Crows

"Saira Viola's work fuses noir glam and disco with the proper sound of the streets. She's a relentless & dedicated adventurer for the story, poem, and novel. A writer whose work creates a star sourced punkish take on the human condition. Her work is a whirlwind of larks & linguistics and the dark & light in between" - David Erdos, Actor, Writer & Director

"A great amount has been done in literature over the years but every now and then someone comes along and shows us a completely different approach to the ancient art of the scribe. So hail Saira Viola and discover her twisted and beautiful imagination. Literature needs Saira Viola. Her writing is sharp direct and gripping." - Benjamin Zephaniah

"A fresh-faced voice to herald in the apocalypse. Posers beware. This is the real deal." - Jonathan Shaw